HIS PERSONAL
AGENDA

HIS PERSONAL AGENDA

BY

LIZ FIELDING

MILLS & BOON®

First published in Great Britain 2001
Large Print edition 2002
Harlequin Mills & Boon Limited,
Eton House, 18-24 Paradise Road,
Richmond, Surrey TW9 1SR

© Liz Fielding 2001

ISBN 0 263 17274 0

Set in Times Roman 16¾ on 18½ pt.
16-0202-47907

Printed and bound in Great Britain
by Antony Rowe Ltd, Chippenham, Wiltshire

CHAPTER ONE

MATT CROSBY considered the man sitting behind the vast mahogany desk with a certain detachment. Charles Parker was not an easy man to warm to, but he would pay well and Matt had a lot of expenses.

'I don't have to explain the problem to you, Crosby,' he said, sliding a file across the polished acres of mahogany. 'This woman is a troublemaker. She's holding up an important development, something badly needed, and she's got to be stopped.'

Matt wasn't taken in by protestations of concern for the public interest. Charles Parker's only concern was for profit. But he picked up the file and contemplated the photograph of a young woman clipped to the inside cover.

Nyssa Blake. The face that launched a thousand town planning appeals.

She headed the wish list of every property developer in Britain. And they all wished the same thing. That she would go away.

According to the brief biography attached she was a few months shy of her twenty-third birthday, but she was already capable of making Charles Parker reach for the panic button. With good reason. Her track record for forcing developers to 'think again' was impressive.

'She can't be allowed to get away with it,' Parker insisted impatiently.

'No, I suppose not.' After all, if she wasn't stopped soon she might get the crazy idea that she could do anything. Matt had been twenty-two himself once, and just about remembered having ideals and a burning desire to put the world to rights, remembered that youthful sense of invincibility that didn't know when it was beaten. He'd learned the hard way.

Parker glanced at him sharply. 'There's no suppose about it.' Then, 'That file contains just about everything that anyone has ever written about her, and my secretary will give you video tapes…news coverage of her last campaign—'

'An out-of-town shopping park, wasn't it?'

Parker shuddered. 'She brought in a botanist who was supposed to have found some rare species no one had ever heard of and cared even less about.'

'Out-of-town shopping has become very un-PC. The local authority was probably glad of any excuse to stop it.' Parker glared at him and Matt shrugged. 'What do you want me to do?'

'Don't tempt me.' Parker laughed shortly. He was seriously rattled, seriously worried, Matt decided. Well, he'd heard rumours that Parker was having cash-flow problems. Any delay would hurt him badly. 'What I'd really like is for someone to shut her up in some deep, dark dungeon and throw away the key.' When Matt was unresponsive to this suggestion Parker shrugged. 'No, well, maybe not.' And he added a little laugh, just to show that he hadn't really meant it.

Matt was not entirely convinced. 'I won't be involved in anything like that,' he said.

'Who would? As well as being the darling of the media, a myth in her own lifetime, she also has some powerful family connections.' He nodded towards the file. 'It's all there. See what you can do with it.'

The file was certainly a hefty one, but Matt Crosby put it back on the desk. 'I'm sure she's a serious pain in the backside but I just don't see what you expect me to do about it. I know some of her hangers-on can get a bit out of hand, but she's a perfect Miss Goody Two-Shoes from all accounts. Never puts a foot wrong.'

'Well, if she's looking for evidence that the Gaumont Cinema at Delvering is worth saving she'll have to break in to find it.'

'Maybe you should just give her a guided tour, show her that she's wasting her time? Maybe you should just bulldoze the place down?' Parker didn't respond to any of those suggestions. Matt shrugged. 'Well, I suppose a court appearance would tarnish the halo...'

'If you think I'm paying your kind of fees just to see her get a fifty-pound fine and a ticking off at the local magistrates' court, you can think again.'

'Faced with a brick wall,' Matt pointed out, 'you have two choices—bang your head against it, or take it down brick by brick.'

Parker snorted. 'I haven't got time for games. This is urgent.' He leaned forward. 'You come highly recommended as a troubleshooter, Crosby. This girl is trouble and I want her...' He hesitated.

'Shot?' Matt offered helpfully.

Parker glared at him. 'Out of my hair. You're supposed to be some kind of genius at digging up those nasty little secrets people would rather keep buried—'

'You make a lot of enemies that way.' Matt looked at the solemn-faced young woman in the photograph. He'd rather make a friend...

The man behind the desk wasn't interested in his problems. 'If you dig deep enough there's got to be something, and once the fawning masses discover that their heroine has feet of clay she'll find the world is a very lonely place.'

Matt did not find the prospect of digging around in Nyssa Blake's life looking for dirt in the least bit appealing. 'This girl is twenty-two years old, Parker, and ever since she dropped out of university she's spent her time stopping people like you riding roughshod over planning regulations. What the devil do you think I'm going to find?'

'What about drugs? All those hippie types smoke pot, don't they?'

'Do they?' He shrugged. 'She's no hippie, Parker. Besides, I doubt that she smokes anything.' He regarded Parker steadily, keeping his features expressionless. 'I'm sure she'd tell you that smoke is bad for the ozone layer.'

The man scowled back at him. 'Sex, then.'

'Sex?' Matt unclipped Nyssa Blake's photograph from the file and stared at it for a moment. She gazed back at him with frank speedwell-blue eyes that looked out from a small oval face framed by a tiny pageboy bob of bright red hair. Her skin was clear and fresh, her mouth full but without a hint of a smile. She had the earnest look of a crusader about her.

There was nothing conventionally beautiful about Miss Nyssa Blake, but he didn't doubt that when she entered a room every eye in the place would swivel in her direction.

'I wouldn't rely on sex to put people off,' he said. On the contrary, he was sure that any suggestion that the lady was free with her favours would have every red-blooded male in the country clamouring to join her action group. 'I should think money is your best bet. Who's putting up the money for her campaigns? Quality PR doesn't come cheap. And the kind of coverage she attracts suggests there's someone behind it who knows what they're doing.'

'Donations from well-wishers, according to the lady.'

'That's a lot of good wishes.'

'We seem to be working on the same wavelength at last, Crosby.' Parker sat back, a small, satisfied smile momentarily straightening his thin lips. 'And if you draw a blank on the money side of things maybe you should take a look at her family. Her father was a soldier, killed in the Gulf War and posthumously decorated for bravery. I'm sure his daughter would do anything to protect his good name. And the dead can't sue for libel.'

'You can make up your own lies, Parker, you don't need me for that.'

'Lies won't do. Even rumours need a little fuel to feed on if they're going to do any damage; I need something with at least a grain of truth to glue it together. If you come across any suggestion of other women or money problems in her father's life, I want to know. Do you understand?' Parker didn't wait for a reply, taking his understanding for granted. And Matt Crosby understood. He didn't much like it, but he understood. 'Her mother remarried three or four years ago,' Parker continued, then paused. 'Her new husband is James Lambert. He's a property developer, too,' he added, thoughtfully tapping the file. 'Nyssa Blake dropped out of university at about the same time. That might be an angle worth pursuing. You've got plenty of material to work with—'

'It's quality that counts, not quantity.'

'Everyone has something to hide, Crosby. Something that wouldn't look too good on the front page of the tabloids. If you can't find anything on the girl, maybe you can dig up some dirt on her family. There are a couple of stepsisters; one is an actress… I just need a lever. I can apply the pressure myself.'

'If she doesn't like the man her mother married she's hardly likely to back off to protect him or his daughters. Why don't you just ask her what she wants from you, Parker? It would save time and money in the long term.'

'Wants?'

'Well, she knows that she's not going to win in the end. You're going to tear down a past-its-sell-by-date cinema and replace it with a supermarket. Maybe a few locals have gone all dewy-eyed with nostalgia, remembering their lost youth spent in the back seats of the stalls, but most of the town would probably rather have the supermarket. All she can do is delay you.'

'All? Every day that passes is costing me—' He stopped abruptly but Matt didn't need to be drawn a picture. The rumours were true; if Parker didn't get the redevelopment of the site through the local planning committee quickly, he was going to be in serious trouble.

'So why not ask her what she wants? You never know, keeping the original façade might do it. Try reason, be accommodating. And if you can smile while you're doing it you might discover that you've become the hero and Miss Nyssa Blake will be the one who has to convince her supporters that she hasn't sold out.'

'That's an excellent idea, Crosby. Unfortunately the supermarket has a corporate image; art deco Gaumont style doesn't even come close. Besides, Nyssa Blake wants the whole thing restored to its former glory. She believes the town needs an entertainment centre more than it needs a new supermarket.'

'Is it? Needed?' Parker gave him a sharp look, but since Matt hadn't expected a straight answer he carried on. 'Look, this isn't a six-lane highway being bulldozed through a site of scientific interest. It's just a local battle with the planners. Small stuff. The media will soon lose interest.'

'You think so?' Parker, for the first time since Matt had entered the room, smiled with genuine amusement. 'I wish I shared your confidence. It might be small stuff, Crosby, but Miss Blake is small in the manner of a mosquito—annoying as hell and quite capable of administering a lethal bite.'

'Maybe you should call the local pest exterminator.'

'I have. You.'

'You've been misinformed. I'm considered something of pest myself—'

'Even pests have to eat, and since I'm reliably informed no one in the City is going to employ you within the foreseeable future...' He shrugged. 'I'm not so fussy, and if you find something on the girl that I can use there'll be a bonus on top of your fee.' The fee he mentioned was substantial, but nowhere near enough.

'Your informants are out of date, Parker. You'll have to double that,' Matt countered, then smiled briefly. 'Inflation,' he offered. Parker said nothing, and Matt had the uncomfortable feeling that he could have asked for more and still have got it. 'I'll want ten days' payment in advance before I start, nonrefundable, and my expenses will be what I need to do the job. No more, no less, no quibble.' He might not particularly relish this job, but right now he couldn't afford to be picky; he had research of his own to finance. 'And no dirty business,' Matt added, just to reinforce what he'd said earlier about Nyssa Blake being locked in a dungeon with the key thrown away.

'You think a lot of yourself, Crosby.' Not true. He thought the chance of finding dirt that would stick to Miss Nyssa Blake rated alongside winning the National Lottery, or the discovery of a hoard of Celtic gold jewellery beneath the concrete yard at the rear of his flat, or even a credit balance in his bank account. All things were possible...but the odds were against it. 'Cash isn't a problem, is it? I'd prefer to keep this unofficial.' Parker took a pack of banknotes from a small concealed safe.

'So long as the ink's dry,' Matt replied wryly, taking one of the notes and flicking it through his fingers as if testing its veracity. 'It all goes through my books—' his enemies would enjoy seeing him on the wrong side of an Inland Revenue audit '—but what you do this end is no concern of mine.' He stowed the money about the pockets of his suit, picked up the file and nodded. 'You'll be hearing from me.'

Image is everything. Nyssa had learned that at her first press conference. Eighteen years old, her hair had been cropped punk-short then, henna-bright against the hastily applied ivory-pale make-up, the black dress borrowed for the occasion from one of her stepsisters.

It had been pure drama and the press had loved her for it. She'd learned a lot that day about image and what it could do for a cause, and she'd abandoned charity store cast-offs and taken on the establishment on its own terms. These days there were developers who backed away from anything she showed an interest in. People took her seriously.

Presumably Charles Parker had thought a neglected cinema would be beneath her notice.

Image. Nyssa stared at her reflection in the mirror. She'd grown out the cropped hair to the briefest of sleek pageboy bobs, but it was still bright red. These days, though, the effect was the result of regular visits to a Knightsbridge crimpers rather than the enthusiastic use of her mother's dressmaking shears and a packet of henna.

Her naturally pale complexion was accentuated by bright red lips that rarely smiled. And now that solemnity too was part of her image.

She sprayed herself with her favourite scent, with its luscious green topnote of gardenia, and turned to the elegant designer dress hanging over the wardrobe door. Black. Of course.

Fine jersey, smooth and flowing as silk. Taking the dress down from its hanger, she lifted it over her head, sliding her arms into long, narrow sleeves, easing the bodice against her skin and letting the skirt fall in a gentle swirl about her legs. She fastened tiny buttons over breasts lifted and emphasised by a black lace bra, the kind of bra that had caused traffic accidents when the advertising hoardings went up.

She was well aware that the effect was sexy as well as dramatic. It had been planned that way. Short of World War Three breaking out, that glimpse of cleavage would guarantee her a place on the front page of every tabloid tomorrow morning.

She'd learned a lot in three years of campaigning. More than how to walk past a security guard and have him hold open the door for her even as she breached his defences. More than how to convince cynical reporters that she was right. More than how to stick it out when she appeared to be the only person in the whole world who cared...

As she fastened a pair of antique jet drops to her earlobes, there was a tap at the door.

'Nyssa?'

Her hands trembled as she was seized by nerves and she nearly dropped one of the precious earrings, fielding it with fingers that were suddenly all thumbs. Damn! She hung onto the edge of her dressing table for a moment, taking slow, careful breaths until she recovered. Then she carefully fastened the second drop, painted a smile on her face and opened the door.

'Gil!' She tried to keep the heartleap out of her voice. Since her group had grown so loud and annoyed so many important people, her brother-in-law had been trying to get her to use one of the specially trained drivers from his security company. So far she had managed to resist him, but on occasion Gil would turn up before a big event to 'offer her a lift'. And his home was not more than twenty or so miles away from the bustling market town of Delvering. 'How unexpected,' she said, managing just a touch of irony. 'Just passing, were you?'

'Not exactly. But I thought you might welcome a little moral support.'

Moral support was the last thing she wanted from her brother-in-law. 'I have the uncomfortable feeling that, roughly translated, that means you still think I'm a little girl who has bitten off a chunk more than she can chew. Right?'

She longed for him to deny it, but he just laughed. 'I might think it, but I wouldn't dare say it. Not the way you're looking tonight.'

'Really?' She hated his laughter, but she'd learned not to let her feelings show around Gil; it wasn't his fault that she was in love with him, so she kept her voice light. 'Was that a compliment? I couldn't be quite sure.'

'Don't fish, brat. You'll have every man in the country leering over your picture in the papers tomorrow. Isn't that enough?'

No. Of course it wasn't. There was only one man she had ever wanted to leer at her. Unfortunately he was married to her stepsister.

'Only if it encourages them to write to the Department of the Environment and demand a planning enquiry,' she said briskly. 'Is Kitty with you?'

'No, Harry's got the sniffles and you know how she fusses about him, but she sends her love.' He paused. 'Actually, she's a bit tired...' Nyssa, not exactly panting to hear about his domestic life, smiled politely and made a move towards the door. Gil put his hand on her arm, stopping her. 'I wanted you to be the first to know, Nyssa. She's expecting another baby.'

He had wanted to tell her himself. Before someone else did. That was why he'd come tonight.

He'd never said a word, yet it was obvious that he knew all about the schoolgirl crush she'd had on him. A friend of her father's, albeit a younger one, he had tried to be kind, walking on tiptoe around her feelings, taking care not to hurt her. It was why he still treated her like a schoolgirl, because he suspected, as Kitty did, that it wasn't just a schoolgirl crush. Well, it couldn't be, could it? She wasn't a schoolgirl any more; she was twenty-two. And kindness was the last thing she wanted from him.

'I'm very happy for you both,' Nyssa said, brightly enough. 'Have you told James and Sophia?' She hadn't been able to bear calling her mother anything but Sophia since she had married Kitty's widowed father—the memory of her own father was still too precious. 'You're going down for James's birthday, I imagine?' Nyssa asked.

'We thought we'd tell everyone then. You'll be there, won't you?'

'If I can,' she hedged. 'The feeling is that Parker will attempt to demolish the cinema quickly, before we can get it listed.' She frowned. 'He's been very slow off the mark.'

'Sophia will be terribly disappointed if you don't come,' Gil said, distracting her. 'We could give you a lift down if you don't want to drive yourself.'

'No. I'll try. Really.' And then she'd discover something desperately important to do. The alternative was to go and smile and hide her feelings, as she had been doing ever since Gil and Kitty's wedding. Except that if she stayed away Kitty would know why and feel sorry for her. And her mother would know why and worry about her. And Gil would know why and feel guilty. She couldn't win. But at least she had an excuse to send him away now. 'You shouldn't be here, Gil. You should be at home with Kitty.'

'She wanted me to come. She worries about you, too, Nyssa.'

Did he really think that knowing his wife had sent him would help? 'The entire Lambert clan appear to have cornered the worry market on my behalf, but it really isn't necessary. I'm among friends here, Gil. The worst thing that's going to happen is the slide projector jamming in the middle of my presentation.'

As if to confirm the truth of her words, someone beat a lively tattoo on the door. 'Nyssa? Are you ready? We're all down in the bar waiting for you.'

'I'll be right with you, Pete. Get me an orange juice, will you?'

'Who's that?' Gil asked. 'Your boyfriend?' He sounded hopeful.

'Boyfriend?' She laid her hand against her breast and managed a laugh. 'What a quaint, old-fashioned word. You might still think of me as a schoolgirl wearing pigtails, Gil, but in case you hadn't noticed I'm all grown up.'

'Actually I had noticed. In that dress it's impossible not to,' he added, dryly. Then, 'So why don't you give your mother a treat and bring him home for the weekend?'

Pete, stick-thin and with a stud through his nose, would hardly be her mother's idea of a treat, she thought. But if she had a man with her it would help to defuse the tension that seemed to be in the air whenever she and Gil were in the same room. 'I'll make a deal with you, Gil. I'll come to the party, and maybe I'll oinvite a friend for the weekend, but only if you stop fussing and go home. Right now.' Please. Before I do something stupid like cry.

Matt was impressed. He'd watched the videos of Nyssa Blake's previous press conferences, given to him by Charles Parker's secretary, but they had just been snippets, put together to be distributed to the media and to likely supporters groups: the edited highlights.

He was impressed by the professionalism, but sceptical too. The camera could lie and frequently did; a competent editor could make anyone capable of stringing together a coherent sentence look like Churchill on a good day. He wanted to see the woman in action, see how she looked before all the fluffs and fumbles had been edited out. So he had used his contacts and got himself a press pass and an invitation to the campaign launch at the Assembly Rooms in Delvering.

And he was still impressed. The Assembly Rooms were straight out of a Jane Austen novel. Georgian and decaying grandly in the

manner of some great old actress, with charm
and elegance. They would look wonderful on
television. A picture was worth a thousand
words, and this, Nyssa Blake was saying, was
the England they were going to save from the
Philistines. Not quite true, of course, but the
cinema, a masterpiece of art deco design that
should have been cherished, had instead fallen
into the kind of decrepitude that was unlikely
to induce the 'aaaah' factor in the average
viewer.

It seemed to Matt that there were some very
sharp brains handling this organisation. Brains
sharp enough to recognise that an idealistic
young woman would make a great spokesper-
son. Maybe, he thought, as his credentials
were checked at the entrance, Parker had a
point.

'Thank you, Mr Crosby.' He clipped the
identification label to his ancient denim jacket
and took the press pack he was offered by a
well-preserved woman wearing a flowing
dress, her long hair loose about her shoulders

and with a New Age name pinned to her em-
broidered bodice.

'Thank you,' he said, and smiled. 'Sky…'

'Just go through. We'll be starting in a minute or two. There'll be drinks and a buffet
afterwards.'

'That's very generous,' he said, inclined to
linger. He wasn't interested in propaganda; he
wanted gossip. 'Who's paying for all this?'

'Our supporters are very generous.' She
gave him a warm, earth-mother smile. 'Of
course we hope you'll make a donation towards your supper.'

He'd walked right into that one, but he
found himself smiling back, even as he stuffed
twenty pounds of Charles Parker's money into
the tin she offered. 'Is there any chance of an
interview with Miss Blake? After the press
conference?'

She consulted her list. 'You're a freelance,
aren't you?'

'I am, but I have a commission to write a
piece on Miss Blake.' Well, he did. Of course
whether the results ever saw print rather de-

pended on what he unearthed in his investigations.

'It's always difficult to arrange private meetings at this kind of occasion, Mr Crosby...'

'Matt,' he said.

'Matt.' Her smile took on a new depth and he realised he had her undivided attention. Which could be useful. 'Nyssa will be mingling afterwards; maybe you could catch her then? I'm afraid that's the best I can do today. Shall I ask her to call you and arrange a time when you'll be able to talk undisturbed?'

'I'll leave my number.' He produced a card that simply bore his name, and on the back he wrote the number of a new mobile phone acquired for the investigation. She stapled it to a folder, along with half a dozen similar offerings, then turned to a new arrival. 'Can I catch you later?' he suggested. 'For a drink? Maybe you could fill me in on the background?'

'Ten o'clock in the Delvering Arms?' she offered, rather too eagerly.

He really needed to look for a new career, Matt thought as he moved on into the foyer, glancing at the press pack he was holding, complete with glossy colour photographs and 'sound-bite' notes.

The whole thing was well organised and very well attended, he realised as he looked about him. Nyssa Blake was news. It took more than a free glass of wine and a sausage roll to tempt the press pack out of London on a summer's evening.

Even if they had no intention of joining her, their readers were eager to know how this young woman intended to set about stopping the developers in their tracks. Youth and innocence against entrenched power always made a good story.

But apart from the local radio and television crews, who were too busy checking equipment and recording their lead-ins to socialise, the newsmen had gathered in small groups, more interested in the latest media gossip than the blown-up photographs of the cinema in its heyday.

Only three or four latecomers were, like him, looking at the photographs and apparently totally absorbed by the notes pinned alongside them. Except the latecomers weren't totally absorbed. They were giving the appearance of deep interest in the exhibition, but their eyes were everywhere as they checked out the gathering crowd. He recognised the type. Minders. Nothing, it seemed, had been overlooked.

Matt watched them for a few moments and then turned as the inner doors were opened. There were chairs put out in rows, a slide projector in the centre with a screen at the front, and a small lectern with a lamp on a slightly raised dais to the side.

Nyssa Blake clearly wasn't relying on the photographs to get her message across. She had a captive audience and they were going to listen and learn before they got to the free food. Sky began to usher people towards the seats.

Two of the men with the restless eyes took seats on either side of the projector. Another sat in front of the lectern. A fourth leaned against the wall, near the entrance. They were covering all the vantage points.

Matt settled himself in the end seat of the back row and, out of habit, looked about him to check for an alternative exit. If trouble was expected he had no intention of being caught up in it.

Nyssa waited in the corridor behind the main hall, her throat dry, her pulse beating too fast. She was always nervous before a presentation, afraid she wouldn't be good enough…

'Ready?' Sky asked, joining her. 'It's show-time.'

'How many…?'

'It's a good turnout. You're big news these days.'

'Right.' She took a deep breath, opened the door, walked up to the lectern, set to the side of a projection screen, and spread out her notes. For a moment the burble of noise continued and then, as she waited, looking around, acknowledging people she recognised, the room gradually grew quiet. That was when she saw him.

He was sitting right at the back, almost as if he didn't want to be there. She knew most of the journalists who covered this kind of story but, wearing antique 501s, and with a mop of thick dark hair that looked as if it had been combed with his fingers, he didn't look like any kind of small-town newspaper man she'd ever met. He looked like a man made for a much bigger stage. Casual he might be, but he made the elegant main hall of the Assembly Rooms look small.

She was smaller than he had imagined from her photographs, and reed-slim, but the neat burnished cap of bright hair, the pale delicate skin, the elegant black dress were pure drama, and every eye in the room was fixed on her, waiting for her to speak.

Matt was not easily impressed, nor, he suspected, were the journalists who had gathered there, and yet he felt a quickening in the air, a stir of anticipation as she looked around the room, acknowledging acquaintances with the briefest of smiles.

Then her gaze came to rest on him, lingering in a look that seemed to single him out, to hold his attention, and just for a second he had the disconcerting sensation that she could see right through him, recognise him for what he was.

He had wondered, looking at her photograph in Parker's office, if her eyes could really be that impossible shade of blue, or whether, like her hair, the colour had been enhanced for effect.

But there was no need to enhance anything. The effect came from something that lit her from within and he knew what it was. Passion.

And her look, he discovered, as for just a moment their gazes locked and held, had a kick like a mule.

Matt hadn't been affected in that way by a woman since Lucy Braithwaite had kissed him in the vestry after choir practice, cutting short a promising career as a solo treble.

He was still struggling to recover his breath when Nyssa Blake took a sip of water before finally beginning to speak.

'Ladies and gentlemen, thank you all for coming to Delvering today,' she began.

Her voice, unexpectedly low and slightly husky, rippled through him, stirring the small hairs at the nape of his neck. Was that how she did it? How she drew supporters to her, twisted cynical newspaper hacks around her dainty fingers, walked past security guards without let or hindrance? Did she just turn on the lamps behind her eyes, murmur in that low voice and turn them into her willing slaves?

He rubbed his hand over his face in an attempt to pull himself together. He hadn't come to the press conference to join the Nyssa Blake fan club. He simply wanted to get the measure of the girl...woman...

Well, he was doing that all right. But it sure as hell wasn't what he had expected.

'I do hope you have all taken advantage of this opportunity to look around Delvering, to talk to local people, to discover for yourselves what exactly is at stake here,' she continued. Then quite unexpectedly she grinned, and for a moment he saw the girl, still there behind the sophisticated veneer. 'But don't worry if you haven't,' she said, indicating the projector with a wave of her hand. It was a gesture that would have done justice to a geisha, controlled, exquisitely graceful, and for just a moment his body seemed to do a loop-the-loop as he imagined what that hand could do to him. 'I'm about to enlighten you, so save your questions until after the show.'

There was a murmur of laughter as the light dimmed until there was just a small shaded lamp over the notes on the lectern, the powerful beam from the projector directing all eyes to the screen with its aerial view of the small market town of Delvering.

As if this was a prearranged signal, several people leapt to their feet in the darkness. There was an angry yell that turned into a cry of pain from the man standing by the projector as it was overturned, hitting the floor was a crash that blew the lamp, plunging the room into darkness.

The heavies. He didn't have to see them to know. He'd recognised them for what they were, despite their suits and their careful interest in Nyssa Blake's work, and he'd assumed they were minders. He'd been wrong.

And there was one right in front of the lectern.

Without pausing to consider the wisdom of his actions, Matt Crosby hurled himself towards the shaded light that illuminated nothing but Nyssa Blake's small hands, frozen in the act of turning over the first page of her notes.

CHAPTER TWO

STARTLED by the crash, Nyssa looked up. The room was dark beyond the small circle of light illuminating her notes and for a moment she froze. Then, as her confused wits began to make some sense of the sounds coming out of the darkness, she began to move.

Too late.

She stepped straight back into the waiting arms of a man who, as he seized her from behind, clamped his hand over her mouth, cutting off her instinctive shout for help.

Matt was still feet away when she let out a startled protest, instantly muffled, and it didn't take much imagination to supply a picture of a large hand covering her face, a burly arm pinning her arms as she was lifted from her feet.

Surging forward, Matt carried them both down onto the floor and, just to make sure he'd got the message, crashed his fist into the man's nose. It was something he'd regret later, when he had time to feel the pain. But not now. Now he simply had to get Nyssa Blake out of there.

He leapt to his feet and, without stopping to waste time or breath in explanations, caught hold of her as she scrambled up, determined on escape. Assuming he was her attacker, re-newing his assault, she struck out at him and her bunched fist connected with the side of his face as he lifted her to her feet. Ignoring the dizzying blow, not stopping to explain, he shouldered her and carried her through a small door that led into a corridor, blinking in the sudden light.

Ignoring the main entrance, he headed for the rear of the building and burst out into the fading light of the late August evening, crossing to the narrow side street where he'd left his car.

Nyssa Blake was yelling and kicking all the way, but all hell appeared to have broken out on the pavement in front of the Assembly

Rooms and no one was taking any notice. Anyone whose business it was to notice undoubtedly assumed he was the guy now trying to put his nose back together.

Neatly done, Parker, he thought grimly as he opened the driver's door of his car, pushed her in and, still hanging onto her, followed. She immediately stopped struggling, and as his grip was hampered by the awkward angle gave a deft wriggle and escaped his grasp. Matt slammed the door behind him and pressed the central locking switch before she reached the door handle.

Small she might be, but when she turned and lunged furiously at him, nails outstretched, it was all he could do to hold her off. And the mule kick effect wasn't confined to her eyes.

'For crying out loud, will you stop that? I'm not trying to hurt you,' he said sharply, then swore as the toe of her fashionable shoe connected with his shin for a second time. She wasn't listening. As she came at him again he was forced to abandon passive defence and instead grabbed both her arms, pinning them behind her as he dragged her hard against him so that she could no longer strike out. His leg thrown over her, pinning her to the seat, dealt with her feet.

For a moment she continued to struggle furiously. He simply hung on until she realised she was wasting her time. Then she went quite still and opened her eyes to look up at him.

'Okay, you win,' she said huskily, her chest heaving as she gasped for air.

Matt deeply distrusted her sudden surrender. He might have subdued her temporarily, but the minute he let go she would undoubtedly let fly at him. And, having tested him to the point where she knew he wouldn't hurt her, she could let rip without fear of the consequences.

But holding on had its dangers too. Her body was pressed beneath him and he was practically drowning in the deep, dangerous currents of her eyes, in the scent that came from her hair, her skin. And her full red mouth was lifted towards him, unconsciously seductive, but seductive nonetheless.

'This isn't a contest, lady,' he said, more harshly than he had intended, and released her so suddenly that she fell back, her dress halfway to her waist where the buttons had parted. He wanted to look away. He really needed to look away. But he knew the minute he did she would fly at him again. So he swallowed hard and tried not to think about the glimpse of black lace and thighs that would give a monk disturbing dreams. 'For your information I just saved you from being kidnapped.'

'Kidnapped?' Impossibly, her eyes widened further.

'You don't think that the projector fell over all by itself, do you? Or that the guy who grabbed you just wanted to dance?' He didn't elaborate; he was sure she was quite capable of working it all out for herself.

Kidnapped? Everything had happened so quickly. Disruption she could understand. The threat of it was always there. But what would be the point of kidnapping her? After a long pause, when all that could be heard inside the car was the sound of ragged breathing being brought under control—his as well as hers— she said, 'You were at the back of the hall.' He was the man she'd known on sight wasn't just some small-town news hound. 'You must have moved very fast...' She eased up in the seat, aware that he was watching her carefully, as if expecting her to bolt at any moment, and began to rub absently at her wrists. 'Unless, of course, you knew what was about to happen.' Which begged the question...if he wasn't a journalist, what was he? Exactly? 'Who are you? What do you want?'

Her eyes narrowed. They did that pretty spectacularly too, Matt thought. She should be shouting, yelling, screaming for the police. It was what any normal girl would do under the circumstances. Her control was slightly unnerving. He sensed she knew that, was using it to her advantage, waiting for an opportunity to flee the moment his guard was down. That was something he could not allow. Not until he was sure she was out of danger. Her reputation was one thing…but that she might be hurt—or worse—he could not allow.

'I'm a freelance journalist—' it depressed him how easily he said the lie '—and I was hoping for an interview.'

She continued to regard him steadily, as if deciding whether to believe him. 'Couldn't it have waited until after the presentation?' she asked finally, then managed a slightly shaky laugh. 'You didn't have to hijack me, you know. If you'd left your number, I'd have called you.'

He managed a grin. This was one cool lady. 'Maybe I have a tight deadline,' he offered. 'Perhaps now, over a brandy, might be a good time.' He needed one even if she didn't. The feeling was beginning to come back to his knuckles with a vengeance.

She regarded him coolly. 'You think that saving me from being kidnapped entitles you to jump the queue?'

'It seems only fair,' he countered. 'After all, I was in the front of the queue when that thug grabbed you.'

'Maybe you do have a point,' she admitted. 'Shall we retire to the bar of the Delvering Arms?'

He hadn't anticipated such instant agreement; it made him suspicious. And shouldn't she be demanding he take her back to the television cameras so that she could tell the world what had happened?

Needing time to think, he turned his head away, looking back to where a noisy crowd had gathered in front of the Assembly Rooms, with people carrying placards demanding the jobs a supermarket would bring to the town and indicating rather graphically that the protesters should get lost.

'They weren't there ten minutes ago,' he said. 'Where have they come from?'

'Mobs-R-Us?' she suggested, with disdain. 'Does it matter? They've done what they were paid for.' Clearly it was the payment that had earned her disdain, not their methods of protesting.

'At least you're certain of making the evening news,' Matt agreed, and even as he spoke the television cameras were being trained on the angry crowd. 'That'll be good for business.'

Her expression suggested otherwise. 'I'd hoped to put our case in a reasoned and thoughtful manner.'

'Do you want to go back and try again?'

'There's no point. I've lost control of the situation. If I go back they'll just shout me down, drown me out. Besides, I'm not dressed for a scuffle.' She smiled a little. At close quarters the blue eyes were lethal. 'Isn't that why you grabbed me? To keep me out of the way? Give them a free run at this?'

He'd thought he'd convinced her. Clearly he had been kidding himself. 'Weren't you listening?' he demanded, just a little angry that his good deed was not being fully appreciated for the altruistic gesture it was. Considering he was supposed to be on the other side. Was on the other side. Except that when he'd said no dirty business he'd meant it. 'I'm not the one who did the grabbing.' He said it slowly and carefully, just to be certain that she understood. 'Someone else had that dubious pleasure. I simply got you out of there, and precious little thanks I've had for my pains.'

'Thanks he wants,' she murmured sarcastically. 'It's a nice story, Mr...' she glanced at the lapel badge clipped to his collar '...Mr Crosby, but really—'

'It's no story, lady,' he said, flexing his stinging hand and holding it up for her to see. 'I've got the wounds to prove it.'

For a moment she stared at his battered and bloody knuckles. Then frowned. 'You're hurt.'

'That's what happens when you hit someone with your fist, or hadn't you noticed?' He took her hand and looked at it. There was a little bruising on one of the knuckles, nothing worse, but even so when he rubbed the pad of his thumb across them she winced and pulled away. 'You see? Maybe next time I should take a leaf out of your book and use my feet,' he said sardonically. Then he realised that she was shaking. 'Oh, look. It's not that bad, really. It was worth a little pain.'

'I hate violence,' she said, with a long shudder. She could have fooled him, but as the trembling reached her voice he put his arm about her and held her close, absorbing the shudders into his own body.

'To tell you the truth, Miss Blake, I'm not all that keen on it myself,' he said, but with her cheek soft against his neck, her slender body fragile as a bird in his arms, he knew just how easy it would be to seriously damage anyone who would hurt her.

As if sensing some change in him, she looked up. 'Who are you really?' she asked. Then she groaned. 'Oh, wait, I get it. You're one of Gil's tame bodyguards, right?' And she pulled back a little. 'I should have known when he left this evening without making a fuss that he'd covered all possibilities...'

Matt didn't say anything. He'd read the files; he knew well enough that the Gil in question had to be her brother-in-law, or more accurately her stepbrother-in-law, Gil Paton. Invalided out of the army after he had taken a sniper's bullet in the Balkans, he now led a consortium of ex-soldiers in a business covering all kinds of security and protection. It was reasonable enough that he would organise some protection for her, which perhaps was why Matt hadn't thought twice about the minders. She had obviously been resisting the idea, though, which was interesting.

'Okay, Mr Crosby...' She squinted at the label attached to his jacket. 'Matt? Is that really your name?' She made one of those graceful little gestures. 'No, don't answer that, since you won't tell me the truth anyway...' She glanced up at him. 'Okay, Mr Crosby, you've done your job. You can take me back to the hotel now.'

'For the brandy and the interview?'

'I don't drink.'

'Never?'

'Not since I turned eighteen. Before that, of course, it was almost mandatory. A bit like losing your virginity before you go into the sixth form...' Her voice trailed away, and for just a moment he thought she was going to blush, which was interesting. It was clearly a well-used ploy to shock maiden aunts—if such things still existed—but why would she think it would shock him? Why would she even bother to try? His silence seemed to un-nerve her a little. 'Actually, you might be right about that drink.'

'I know I am.' He leaned forward to start his car. 'And it's definitely time we got out of here,' he added, as he glanced in the mirror. 'Unless, of course, you've changed your mind about giving an interview?' With a jerk of his head he indicated the approaching television crew, who were looking for anyone who might have seen something interesting or some local with a point of view to air.

She half turned, hesitated, then shook her head. 'No…'

'You're sure? You could win the sympathy vote right now. A few tears on the pavement will melt hearts of stone. And the glimpse of underwear will ensure you have at least half the country's undivided attention.'

She stiffened, grabbed the front of her dress and began to work on the buttons. 'That's not my style, Mr Crosby.' She caught his questioning look. 'They might have wrecked my press conference but I'll think of some way to turn this to my advantage. I mean, it hardly puts Mr Parker on the side of the angels, does it? It's odd, because I would have thought he was cleverer than that...'

'Maybe he's more desperate than you thought. And you've missed the point.' And a button, but he thought it wiser not to mention that. 'If whoever set this up had been successful, you wouldn't have been around to organise anything.'

She stared at him and he could see the reality of what had happened was beginning to sink in. 'Yes. I see.' She glanced back again. 'Maybe I should—'

'No, you shouldn't. As you said, it's not your style.' Besides which, her lipstick was smudged, her sleek cap of hair uncharacteristically mussed. For a moment she didn't look anything like the controlled, determined young woman who had fearlessly taken on big business and had it on the run. She looked like a girl who, for a moment, was just a little bit lost, and Matt wanted to hold her, reassure her. He managed to stop himself, but it was a close-run thing. 'And if you're at all keen to hang onto your reputation for unruffled perfection in the face of adversity, Miss Blake, I think I should tell you that you could use a comb.'

She lifted her hand to her hair in a self-conscious gesture. 'Oh, right. In that, case, Mr Crosby, I suggest we retire to the bar of the hotel with all speed.'

'Just Crosby will do,' he said as he let slip the handbrake, checked the mirror and moved away from the kerb. 'Or Matt, if you promise to keep your feet to yourself. I don't usually allow people who kick me to get that personal. What do your family call you?' he asked, while she was making up her mind.

'A nuisance?' she offered. 'And I hate to think what the construction industry call me.'

'Much the same,' he said, with a grin. 'But the less printable versions.' And, since he didn't intend listing them, he put his foot down hard and his old Mercedes surged forward, leaving the approaching news hounds standing.

Once out of sight of the Assembly Rooms he slowed, and a few moments later pulled into the staff car park at the rear of the Delvering Arms.

'We'll stick to the back way, I think,' he said, taking her arm and steering her in via the kitchen. He nodded to the chef and headed for the stairs.

Nyssa stopped abruptly. 'I thought we were going to have a drink?' she said.

'We are. But not in the bar. It'll be a bit crowded?' he suggested as her eyebrows hit her hairline.

'In that case I'll still need my key,' she said.

'I'd wait until things have quietened down a bit,' he advised, taking his own key from his pocket.

'But—'

'People will be looking for you. Your room is the first place they'll go.' She still hesitated.

'They may not all have your best interests at heart,' he pointed out.

'I still have my doubts about you,' she said crossly.

She might suspect that he was connected with Paton, but it was obvious that she wasn't totally convinced. It was smart of her to be suspicious, but Matt didn't want her having second thoughts about him now. 'You can call Gil Paton from my room, if you like,' he said, hoping to reassure her.

'Why would I want to do that?'

'Your little skirmish will be on the news later. He might worry.'

'If you're that concerned you can call him yourself.' She turned and headed up the stairs without further argument, giving him a great view of the way her dress clung to her figure, the way the skirt swayed seductively about her hips and legs. She stopped abruptly as she reached the top and he narrowly avoided bumping into her. It wasn't that he didn't want to bump into her. Just that his body had taken enough punishment for one day, both physical and sensual. 'Well?' she demanded, when they reached the top of the stairs. 'Will you call him? Report in? Tell him that he was right? As usual.'

Matt wasn't sure what was irritating her the most—the fact that her brother-in-law thought she needed a bodyguard, or the fact that he had been proved right.

'Why would he listen to me? I've never met the man. My room's this way,' he said, indicating the corridor to the left.

She made a dismissive noise. 'You expect me to believe that?'

He offered a smile by way of reply. 'This is it.' And he slid the key into the lock and held the door open for her. 'And there's the phone. Help yourself. See what he says when you thank him for saving you from...' He stopped. From Parker's deep, dark dungeon? Was the man desperate enough to take a short cut if he thought he might get away with it?

He'd assumed she was just a pretty face to front the group, but now he'd seen her in action, met her, Matt had no doubt that Nyssa

Blake was the driving force behind the campaign to save the cinema.

While there would certainly be a fuss of monumental proportions if she disappeared for any length of time, media attention would shift from the cinema to the hunt for Nyssa, distracting her supporters, leaving them without a leader. And if it could be made to look as if she had been frightened off, had run away...

It shouldn't be beyond the wit or imagination of Charles Parker to arrange sightings of look-alikes in a variety of glamorous places, fostering resentment and anger among those people who had given their time, their energy, their money to her cause. By the time she reappeared, lost and wandering somewhere, dazed from drugs, or worse, it would all be over.

And if he went to the police with his suspicions what could he tell them? That Parker had given him a wad of money to find out something bad about the girl? Parker would deny it and Matt had no proof. And Nyssa would be the first to admit that the police were not her number one fans. They'd probably be as relieved to see the back of her as the developers.

It occurred to him that the sooner he found something to use against her, something that might at least pressure her into moderating her demands, the better. It wasn't pleasant, but it could save her from a lot worse.

'Saving me?' She glanced back at him, prompting him to go on.

He stared at her for a moment, half believing she could read his mind. Then he realised she was referring to his last half-finished sentence, and he managed a shrug. 'From whatever those goons had in store. I'll leave it to your imagination. And while you're making your call, I'll get us a drink.'

'You should clean up your hand first.'

'My hand will wait. The bathroom is through there if you want to freshen up,' he said, heading for the minibar and hunkering down to examine its contents.

'This is a lovely room. Much bigger than mine.'

'I'm on expenses. Besides, it was all they had left.'

'Expenses?'

You've got a big mouth, Crosby. Or maybe she'd hit him harder than he realised. 'I've got a commission,' he said. 'If you want your picture in full glossy colour on a magazine cover, I'm your man.'

There were a couple of brandy miniatures in the fridge. Right at that moment he could have used both of them himself, but he poured them into two glasses, then picked one up and took a mouthful, letting its heat wash slowly over his tongue before he swallowed it. He turned and realised that Nyssa hadn't moved, but was standing watching him. He picked up the other glass and carried it over to her. She didn't take it. 'You really should clean up your hand,' she insisted.

He tightened his fist to assess the damage. 'I'll live.'

'I don't doubt it. Nevertheless...' When he didn't move, she made an impatient little noise with her tongue, took both glasses from him and set them down on a small table. 'Come on. I'll do it for you.'

'There's no need, Miss Blake—'

'Nyssa,' she said abruptly. Then, 'I do hope you're not going to make a fuss. I can't stand men who make a fuss.' Before he could deny even thinking of such a thing, she had taken him by the wrist and was leading him firmly towards the bathroom.

'You're incredibly bossy for such a little thing,' he said.

'Of course I'm bossy.' And quite suddenly she smiled. Really smiled. 'How far do you think I'd get if I went around saying "please" and "may I?" and "do you mind?", all the time?'

'Not far,' he muttered, still trying to come down from the effect of her smile, desperately hoping she wouldn't notice the way his body was responding. It had been touch and go since he'd first set eyes on her. Now, pushed up as tight against the door as he could get, he was still far too close to Nyssa Blake as she filled the sink with warm water, and the long, pale curve of her neck was an invitation to a soft caress…

'Take your jacket off.'

'Bossy,' he said, but his voice caught a little in his throat and he turned away to peel off his denim jacket. She took it from him and hung it behind the door. Then he swallowed hard and stared at the ceiling as she took his hand between hers and submerged it in the warm water.

'Does it hurt?' she asked.

'Like hell,' he said, because that was what she expected. He wished it did, at least it might distract his rampaging libido long enough for him to get it back under control. But the stinging was easily counteracted by the gentle touch of her fingers. Matt had the feeling that he could undergo major surgery without anaesthetic if Nyssa Blake held his hand.

'There, that should do it.' She pulled the plug and the water ran away. She pulled a small towel from the rack and gently dried his hand and fingers, dabbing away a tiny ooze of blood that seeped from a graze.

He could have stayed there all night while she did it. Not a good idea. The bathroom was too small and she was too close.

'Thanks,' Matt said, somewhat abruptly. 'That'll do it.' He pulled the door open and headed swiftly in the direction of his brandy, draining it in one swallow.

'Does it hurt that much?'

'What?' He turned to find Nyssa watching him with a slightly perplexed frown creasing her smooth forehead. God, he was handling this badly. 'Oh. No. It's fine now. You've got the gentle touch.'

'Yes, well, you get used to dealing with cuts and abrasions when you're in this business. Security guards aren't too bothered about where they put their bolt-cutters when you've chained yourself to a bulldozer.'

'I didn't think you got involved in anything like that.'

'When needs must,' she said, with a careless shrug.

He barely stopped himself from saying something stupid, something patronising along the lines of How did a delicate little creature like you get involved in something like this? She might look fragile, but he was still feeling the kicks she had given him. Patronising might just get him another one. And this time he would deserve it.

'Are you planning on chaining yourself to the front door of the cinema?'

She gave him a thoughtful look. 'That depends on Mr Parker.' Then, as if to demonstrate that was all she was prepared to say on the subject, she turned and picked up the brandy he had poured for her. She sipped it, then pulled a face and handed it to him. 'I knew there was a reason I didn't drink. Here, I think you need this more than I do. Can I make myself a cup of tea?'

'Help yourself,' he invited, and she moved across the room to the kettle, busying herself with a cup and a teabag while she waited for it to boil. 'There are some biscuits in my bag if you're hungry.'

'Biscuits?'

'Chocolate ones. You never know when you're going to have to miss out on the canapés...'

'Feel free to go back and help yourself, Crosby,' she said irritably. 'I'd hate you to miss out on a free beanfeast.'

He remembered the twenty pounds he'd donated. Hardly free, but he let it pass. 'You think there'll be anything left? I imagine the rent-a-mob crowd will have taken the booze and trashed the food.' Nyssa Blake swore, briefly but comprehensively. 'Is that the kind of language that they taught you at the school for young ladies you went to?' he asked. 'The Sacred Heart, wasn't it?' She stared at him. 'You see, Nyssa, I've done my homework on you.'

'You mean you really are a journalist?'

'One with a scoop,' he replied, avoiding the direct lie this time. It was a bit late, but he was doing his best.

'Oh, sure,' she said as the kettle boiled. 'Big story.' She dropped a teabag into a cup and filled it with water. 'Nyssa Blake had a cup of tea in my bedroom after a scuffle at the Assembly Rooms. I offered her a biscuit—no, wait—' she held up a small hand for attention '—a chocolate biscuit, but she declined. She drank her tea and left shortly afterwards.'

Matt laughed. 'You'd better stick to bulldozer-bashing, Nyssa, if that's the best you can do with this story. You'll certainly never make a journalist.'

'I have no wish to be a journalist.'

'You planned to read English at university,' he pointed out.

'Yes, well, there's not much future in that.' She discarded the teabag and after a tussle with a tub of milk finally managed to open it and pour it into her tea. Then, looking at him out of the corner of her eye, she said, 'Okay, so tell me, how would a big freelance journalist like you handle the story?'

She said that as if she still didn't buy the journalist bit, but Matt, leaving the armchair for Nyssa, ignored the disbelief in her voice and stretched out on the bed. 'Broadsheet or tabloid?'

'Oh, let's go for broke. Give me tabloid.'

He grinned and sipped thoughtfully at the brandy for a moment. 'How about this. "Tonight, before a room packed with journalists, a daring attempt was made to kidnap Nyssa Blake. The dazzling redhead—"' Nyssa snorted '"—the dazzling redhead, twenty-two-year-old stepdaughter of millionaire businessman James Lambert, was grabbed on the point of launching her campaign to stop the destruction of the art deco Gaumont Cinema. Opened in Delvering in 1931 by home-grown silent screen star Doris Catchpole—"' Nyssa reprised the snort, except that this time it came closer to a giggle '"—the Gaumont is due to be demolished by developers and replaced by a supermarket."' He took another sip of the brandy. ' ' 'The meeting had only just started when, as the lights dimmed for a slide presentation, the projector was overturned and smashed and Miss Blake was grabbed by an unknown assailant. Matt Crosby, thirty-four, freelance journalist, fought off her attacker and in the confusion carried Miss Blake to safety. Later, comforted by her rescuer in the safety of his hotel bedroom—' ' '

'Oh, right, I get it—'

' ' '—his hotel bedroom,' ' ' Matt continued firmly, ' ' 'Miss Blake bathed Mr Crosby's injuries and wept, devastated by what had happened—' ' '

'Stop it, Matt Crosby, journalist, aged thirty-four. That's quite enough.'

'You didn't like it?'

'I'd have to give you an E for effort, I suppose—'

'Only an E?'

'That's all you deserve. You used far too many long sentences for the tabloids. But you're clearly quite twisted enough to be a journalist. It would definitely be a U for accuracy.'

'A U?' he queried.

'Ungraded.'

'It's nothing but the unvarnished truth,' he protested.

'Really? What about the fictitious Doris Catchpole?' she demanded. 'And when did I weep or say I was devastated by what happened this evening?'

'Oh, that. Just a little poetic licence.' He grinned. 'You wouldn't want me printing what you actually did say, would you? Not that a family newspaper would actually print the words, just the first letter and then some asterisks, but the great reading public would get the general idea...'

'I'll bet they would.' She gave him a thoughtful look. 'I don't think I like you very much, Matt Crosby.'

'It's just a job, Nyssa. It's nothing personal.' He offered her the brandy glass. 'Changed your mind about that drink?'

'Yes. And the interview.' She abandoned her tea and headed for the door. 'I can't say that it's been nice knowing you...it hasn't.' She swept into the tiny vestibule and out of sight. He heard her flip the latch. Then, 'Oh, hell!'

'What's up?' he asked as she retreated back into his room.

'There's a crowd of journalists camped outside my bedroom door.'

'In a hotel of this quality? I'm shocked.'

Nyssa glared at him. He was having considerable difficulty in keeping a straight face, she realised. 'No, you're not,' she said. 'You think it's funny.'

He didn't deny it. 'But not entirely unexpected. In fact I seem to remember warning you that it was likely. Of course,' he said, more soberly, 'there's always the possibility that not all of them are journalists. Did they see you?'

'No. They were concentrating on the stairs.'

He relaxed, leaning back against the thickly padded headboard. 'It'll have to be the fire escape, then. It's along the hall.' He put down the glass and laced his fingers behind his head. 'Oh, no. That won't do. They'll all see you leaving my room. Oh well, never mind. It will give credence to my scoop.'

'It won't be a scoop,' she pointed out with a certain amount of satisfaction. 'Not if they all have the story.'

'But I'll be writing it from the inside.'

She said something rude. Then, a little desperately, 'You could leave without anyone noticing and let me stay here tonight. And if you were a gentleman you wouldn't say a word to anyone.'

'That's true.' If he were a gentleman he wouldn't be having the kind of thoughts that were racketing through his head right now. But if her assailants were determined enough she would be a whole lot safer with him tonight. 'But I thought we'd already agreed that I was a journalist. The one surely precludes the other? And you wouldn't throw me out into the cold, cold night, would you? Not after I've risked life and limb to save you.'

'It isn't a cold, cold night. It's still August—just. And I'm sure the hotel will be able to fix you up with something—'

'You're missing the point, Nyssa. If I leave this room it would only take half a brain to work out why.' He shifted across to the side of the bed and patted the space beside him. 'But you're most welcome to stay.'

'Asterisk you, Matt Crosby,' she said, then crossed to the window, throwing the casement wide open. The door wasn't the only exit.

CHAPTER THREE

MATT CROSBY'S room was at the side of the hotel, situated over a quiet side street. Unlike the hotel corridor it was deserted, and the first floor wasn't so very far from the ground. If she'd been dressed in practical clothes and a pair of boots Nyssa wouldn't have thought twice about swinging over the sill and risking the drop.

But she was wearing a designer dress that might have cost a small fortune but didn't offer much by way of protection from a rolling fall. And her shoes had little to commend them but fashion. Added to which her car keys were in her handbag, along with her wallet, lost in the scuffle at the Assembly Rooms. No doubt someone would have picked it up. She just hoped it was a friendly someone.

Which reminded her that she really should call Sky to reassure her that she was safe. But the thought didn't appeal very much. In truth, the idea depressed her. She and Sky had been getting further and further apart with each campaign and Nyssa just wasn't in the mood for a long 'I told you so' lecture on the stupidity of offering herself up as a target.

The thought of a reverse charge call to Gil from the local phone box didn't hold a lot of charm either. He wouldn't actually say, I told you so, but she'd be able to hear him thinking it. And he'd come and take her back to his cottage and Kitty. Definitely not an option...

She glanced back at Crosby. Heavy lids hooded his eyes but she knew that he was watching her, just as she sensed that she only had to ask him for help and he would give it. He was simply teasing her. She was almost sure he had been teasing her about the story he would write, too. Almost. It was so long since anyone had teased her she couldn't be quite sure she was reading the signs right.

Her father had used to tease her all the time. Gil too. But her father was dead and

Gil…well, he'd stopped teasing her about the same time he'd met Kitty.

'Well, are you going to jump for it?' Matt Crosby asked, after a while.

'What's it to you?' she retaliated edgily.

'Nothing. But I'd be grateful if you'd hurry up and make up your mind. There's a bit of a draught from that window.'

'You are—' she began, but he cut her off.

'I know, but shut the window. I'm susceptible to cold.'

'It's not in the least bit cold.'

'Then I must be shivering at the thought of what could happen when you hit the pavement. I'm a bit squeamish that way.' Not exactly teasing. But his words still gave her a ridiculously warm feeling. The kind of feeling that might, if a girl wasn't careful, end in tears. She turned away, quickly, but he got up and crossed to the window, looking down at the pavement for a moment before closing it for her. 'It's a long way down, Nyssa,' he said gently, as she began to protest. 'You'll be safe enough here.' He pulled the curtains across, shutting out the deepening twilight before switching on a lamp. 'I promise.' Then he turned and looked down at her with the kind of even grey eyes that made you feel safe.

Safe? Cherished? Tears even? Whoa, girl, just what is going on here? Nyssa asked herself. Since when have you wanted to feel safe?

Since someone clamped his hand over your mouth and pinned your arms to your side and you knew, you just knew, you'd gone too far this time: that this time you were not going to get away with it.

Maybe Gil was right. Maybe she did need someone she could rely on. An outsider with no axe to grind, who was there just for her. Matt Crosby insisted he was a journalist, not part of Gil's group at all, and that should have made her feel less safe, not more. But it didn't. He had acted by himself to save her, not because Gil had sent him. That alone made him just a bit special. And he was special. She had recognised that the moment she'd set eyes upon him.

Matt Crosby had that tough, classless look about him, moving easily, as if beneath the jeans and the faded collarless shirt he was really fit. Not heavily muscled, but lean and sinewy and hard as hell. A bit like her father. She wondered if he had ever been a soldier, but she didn't ask him because if he said yes her illusions would be shattered, and she would know that her first guess had been right, that he was one of Gil's chosen men.

It came as something of a shock to realise that she wanted to think that *she* had chosen him.

'A broken leg wouldn't help your campaign, would it?' he said, after a moment.

'What? Oh, no. I suppose not.' Then, 'Those plaster casts can really slow you down. Matt?'

The way she said his name tugged at something deep, long buried. 'Yes?' he asked, somewhat hoarsely.

She glanced up at him. 'What kind of story did you plan to write about me?'

Since that was part of his cover for getting to meet her, Matt had that one already worked out. 'I was hoping to spend some time with you, with your group. Find out how you set about making life hard for some poor developer. Why? Do you fancy yourself on the cover of a glossy magazine after all?'

Not particularly. And the idea was crazy, stupid. Except that maybe, just maybe, this time it would be a good idea to have someone at her side she could rely on in a crisis, the way she'd once felt she could depend on Sky. And if he was writing a big story about her he would be there, at her side, and no one would question it...

Nyssa was suddenly confused, remembering the kick of something hot and sweet in the pit of her stomach when she'd first seen him. She didn't know what she wanted. Or maybe she did. She just didn't want to confront the reality, preferring to cling to something precious, something out of reach. Something safe.

She turned away from him to lean back against the wall. 'It occurred to me that to-night might not be a one-off,' she said. 'It was all very well organised, don't you think?'

Matt thought about the four men who had positioned themselves to strike the moment the lights went out. 'I'd say they knew what they were doing,' he agreed.

'And it was just luck that you were there?'

'Yes.'

She gave a little shiver. 'You're right, it is cold.'

'You should have had that brandy. Or, failing that, hot sweet tea.' He picked up the cup, then put it down again. 'You've let it go cold. That just leaves bed.'

'Bed is impossible too,' she said. 'My room is staked out by a gang of reporters who won't give me a bit of peace…'

'Forgive me, but I wasn't under the impression that you were looking for peace.' She didn't answer. 'You could always take mine.'

She looked up at him, not quite sure what he was offering. 'Your room?'

'My bed,' he said, and she realised that while he might—just—be willing to take the armchair if she insisted, he wasn't about to vacate his room and leave her in sole possession.

She opened her mouth to protest. Then she closed it. Then she swallowed and said, 'But I can't stay here all night...'

'Why not? You'd share a night watch with me, wouldn't you? Chained to that art deco staircase to stop Parker's men tearing it down?'

'That isn't the same.' It was his turn to remain silent, but she sensed the tenseness in him, saw the heat darken his eyes. He knew it wasn't the same, and in the silence desire stirred the air like a sultry breeze lifting the leaves in an ancient woodland. It stole through Nyssa's body like some old, dark secret, and licked along her thighs, leaving her weak, trembling...

Could this be it? The moment to put Gil and her childhood feelings behind her? Fear drove passion... That had to be it, she decided, almost with relief. This was an adrenalin charge, nothing more serious than that. Well, that was fine. Perfect, almost. It was emotion that scared her. And slowly she raised her hand to the first of the buttons that fastened her dress.

For a moment she just let her fingers lie there. One button would be all the answer he needed. One tiny jet button. Nothing. Everything.

As she slipped the loop she heard the catch in his breathing and the tiny sound seemed to start something inside her, a quickening, an urgent need to be held in a pair of strong arms, held and loved. Now. This minute. And as she raised her lashes, looked Matt Crosby full in the eyes, she saw an answering need simmering in their depths.

His jaw tightened. 'Nyssa...I didn't mean...'

'Didn't you?' And a second button parted from its loop.

Nyssa could see that he was trying to remain cool, but she knew that one word was all it would take to drive him over the edge. Well, that was good. She wanted him to boil over and take her with him, take her and make her forget...

'Kiss me, Matt Crosby,' she said, her voice hoarse as unshed tears tightened her throat. Four words. That was all. But they were the right four, because with a soft moan he reached out and slid his fingers through her hair, cupping her head in his hand. 'Kiss me,' she repeated recklessly.

Matt knew he should back off, resist the clawing heat of his body. This was breaking all the rules. Don't get too close. Don't get involved. But it was too late for those thoughts. It had been too late ever since Nyssa Blake had stepped onto the podium in the Assembly Rooms.

He had been drawn by something almost desperate in her eyes, a vulnerability, a hunger that had seemed to reach out across the rows of chairs, the gathered journalists, something that had spoken directly to him; the rules had never stood a chance.

Besides, the rules no longer mattered. Parker had broken them first. No dirty business, Matt had said, and he had meant it. What had happened tonight had broken the contract. Tomorrow he'd return Parker's money, even though he had every right to keep it, but he'd give it back and tell him to find someone else to do his dirty work. He'd manage somehow; he always managed...

Then, as Nyssa tilted her face to him with something almost desperate in those lambent blue eyes, he put thinking on hold and started acting. He reached for her, pulled her close, trawling her full, red mouth, tasting her lips, swallowing her scent so that it became part of him for ever.

She must have liked it because she reached up and put her hands about his neck, a gesture at once knowing and trusting, as she dropped all her defences. Emboldened, he let his hand drift down over the sweet curve of her hips, tugging her in tight against him so that she would be in no doubt about what she was doing to him.

Through the heavy cloth of his jeans Nyssa felt the urgency of Matt's desire. His eyes, in that moment when she had first seen him across the length of the Assembly Rooms, had touched a fuse at a moment when she had been feeling low, vulnerable. To know that she was desired, wanted, had set a charge to the banked-up heat of longing that had been simmering for years.

Pain piling on confusion piling on disaster had driven her into the arms of Matt Crosby, and now he was offering her the strength and comfort of his body, a refuge. For a moment she felt again the panic in the sudden darkness when an unknown man's hands had grabbed for her, covering her mouth and nose in a smothering, suffocating nightmare. No one had ever got that close to her before. A shiver of apprehension went through her and she clung to Matt, needing his strength.

She had been the one in control for so long, the one everybody looked to for a lead. Tomorrow they would all clamour for answers, reassurance: the press, her helpers, her family. But for now Matt was offering her a moment out of time, the chance to be just any girl in the arms of any man.

How she had longed for that moment of bittersweet surrender, carrying the pain of her longing deep inside her, hoping that one day Gil would come to her; knowing, deep in her heart, that he never would. To him she was, always would be, his dead friend's little girl. Just as she would always have been a little girl to her father. But Matt didn't think that. He saw her as a woman, a desirable woman. And she shivered.

'This is crazy—' He stopped her protest with a slow, sweet kiss that seemed to sap her will-power and turn her bones to water. She knew that it meant nothing, was simply the flight from danger driving her responses in man's only antidote to death. Yet an excitement shimmered through her, the need to know...

'Madness,' he whispered. But one hand at her nape gentled her while the long square-tipped fingers of the other continued to slip the loops from the tiny jet buttons in a slow, exquisitely intimate disrobing that was heating her skin, firing her own damped-down yearning.

In that first moment when she'd stepped up onto the platform she'd recognised in him the type of man that mothers warned their daughters about. Dangerous. Sexy. The type of man who could make you forget anything. The intensity of his gaze had hooked her attention as she had glanced about the room, holding her, so that for a moment she had found it difficult to look away. It was an intensity that burned bright in him now.

All she knew about him was his name, that he was thirty-four years old and that he was a journalist. And it didn't matter. The world was on hold. Outside of Matt Crosby's hotel room time was standing still. Tomorrow everything would be, if not quite the same, then nearly so. The interviews, the planning, the endless telephone calls would continue even more intensely because of what had happened at the Assembly Rooms. She began to tremble and her legs buckled weakly, so that she leaned against him.

'Nyssa…' She clung to him. 'Nyssa, it's all right. Don't cry. You're safe.' He thumbed the tear from her cheek and he held her and rocked her as the reaction slammed in hard and she wept into his shirt.

'I'm sorry…so sorry…'

'I know, sweetheart. I know.' And he did know. She needed him, needed someone to hold onto in the darkness. But not like this. He gathered her close, held onto her, straining every sinew to hang onto some semblance of sanity. He didn't do this. He didn't have sex with strangers. Except this wasn't just sex. It was more, much more than that. As he held her in his arms, felt the tremor in her limbs, the rapid beat of her pulse beneath his hand, he knew he wanted much more than that. 'You're safe here,' he said. 'I won't let anyone hurt you.' And as she clung to him Matt felt as if he was melting from the inside out. *I won't let anyone hurt you.*

*   *   *

Waking in strange places, situations fraught with danger, had instilled in Nyssa a discipline of stillness, of silence while she sorted out the messages bombarding her brain. As she gradually focused on the man lying beside her this habit did not desert her, despite the rush of memories that rose to her throat and threatened to choke her.

Memories of the way Matt had held her, comforted her, shushed away the demons and made her feel safe.

His thick dark hair was feathered across his forehead and in sleep he had lost much of the hard-edged wariness that marked his mouth. She'd sensed it behind his eyes, even when he'd held her close like a small child as the reaction to everything that had happened to her had finally kicked in and she had clung to him, trembling and weeping.

She had to curl her fingers tight to stop herself from reaching out to him, waking him with the touch of her hand against his lips, the urge to thank him with everything she had to give.

Most men would have taken advantage of the way she had reacted and made love to her. He had not. Which seemed to answer any doubts she might have. He was a good man.

Too good to be true?

The thought rose to taunt her gullibility. No man was that good. So, who was Matt Crosby? Really?

He'd said a journalist, a freelance journalist. Maybe. She could check that. She would check it. Because, despite the ease with which he'd rattled off that parody of a tabloid story last night, he hadn't quite convinced her that writing was his trade. At least, not his primary one. He was too hard, too quick on his feet, too wary.

Obviously he'd got an invitation to the presentation from somewhere; his name would have been checked against a list at the door. They'd had troublemakers gatecrash their press conferences before and learned to be vigilant.

But the man who'd jumped her had got inside too, along with the men who'd smashed the slide projector. Too easily. Infiltration of their ranks wasn't difficult and their enemies were getting smarter.

Were they smart enough to work out that she would trust without question a man who had snatched her from the terror of unknown hands reaching out from the darkness? She watched the man sleeping beside her, remembering the way he had held her through the tears, gentling her with his voice, his tender touch, until she had finally fallen asleep curled up against the comfort of his chest. And she hated herself for doubting him.

And yet… And yet…

There was more than one way to get a man on the inside, just as there was more than one way of keeping a girl a prisoner. She was here, wasn't she? In his room. In his bed. Last night he had been Galahad, her white knight. What would he do if she decided to leave? If she woke him, said, Thanks… See you around…?

Would he pull her into his arms, kiss her as she had begged him to last night, so that she'd forget all about leaving? That she didn't doubt his ability to do just that spoke volumes. Or maybe he'd simply offer to take her home, or anywhere she wanted to go. Perhaps, just as an afterthought, he'd suggest the safe haven of his own home, a place where her enemies could not find her. Wrapped in the silken cords of desire, the warmth of his kindness, she would never suspect that she was a prisoner. And even if she did, she still might not want to escape.

Even as the treacherous thoughts formed in her head Nyssa watched the gentle rise and fall of Matt's chest. She longed to reach out, run her fingers over his smooth sun-darkened skin, have her doubts swept away as he woke and pulled her into the warm curve of his body. It took all her strength not to wake him and grab at the momentary illusion of safety, the momentary illusion that she was loved.

Might not want to escape? Who was she trying to kid? She had to get away right now, before he woke. She forced herself to turn away while she still could and began to ease herself across the bed.

'You've got five minutes, sweetheart.' Matt's voice was heavy with sleep. 'After that, you've got company.'

Nyssa looked back over her shoulder. He hadn't moved, but a glint of grey showed beneath heavy lids as he watched her walk across the room. All that self-denial must have put a strain on his good intentions, and she'd be the first to admit that he'd had a lot of provocation. Even now, the temptation to turn around and go back to bed, to him, dragged at her. She had to get out of there before she abandoned all reason.

Forsaking all idea of retrieving her dress— if she so much as looked in that direction he'd know—she headed purposefully for the bathroom, conveniently situated by the door. She'd slept in his shirt and that would have to do for the dash to her room.

'Five minutes is all I need,' she said briskly, and then was out of his sight in the room's tiny vestibule. The bathroom door was to her left, the door to the corridor ahead.

Nyssa placed one hand on each of the door handles and opened them both at the same time, so that he wouldn't hear a second click, be alerted to her bid for freedom. She wasn't giving him the chance to stop her.

Maybe, though, she should take a towel. She didn't much relish the idea of appearing in Reception in nothing but her knickers and a man's shirt. Just in case anyone from the tabloids was still hanging about. She ducked quickly into the bathroom and used the loo, flushed it, washed her hands—sounds he'd be expecting—before taking advantage of the situation to grab the biggest towel she could find and wrap it around her waist like a sarong.

Then she turned the shower on. It should hold him long enough for her to find a chambermaid to let her into her own room. Except, of course, he wasn't the sort of man you could just walk away from without a word. He would follow her there. And her car keys were in her handbag, lost in the scuffle at the Assembly Rooms.

For just a moment she considered giving up all thought of escape. She would go back, get into bed... Nyssa caught herself, horrified by her thoughts. Last night there had been some excuse for the way she'd thrown herself at him...fear...shock...

To stay now would be...wanton.

It wasn't as if she trusted him. She had to leave. Now. Get away from everyone. She needed time to think. For that she needed transport.

Matt's jacket was still hanging behind the bathroom door and slowly, quietly, she felt in the pocket until her fingers closed around his keys. Escape was no longer a problem. The problem was a lingering desire to stay...

Refusing to be tempted, she wound a second, smaller towel round her head like a turban, to cover her bright hair, and then, taking a deep breath, eased her way carefully out of the bathroom. Her shoes were by the bedroom door, where she had kicked them off last night, and she grabbed them before easing herself out into the corridor, leaving the door slightly ajar. The click of it shutting would be more than enough to alert a man like Matt Crosby.

Ignoring the startled glance of another early riser, she ran lightly in her bare feet along the corridor to her own room, still hoping she might find a chambermaid with a master key so she could grab a handful of clothes before Matt discovered she had gone. But chambermaids were like policemen. There was never one around when you needed one.

The kitchen staff, getting started on breakfast, turned in astonishment as she waltzed through wearing Matt's shirt, a towel and a smile.

'Good morning,' she said brightly. Then she was out into the cool, clean morning air and she slipped on her high-heeled shoes and crossed the car park.

Matt's dark blue Mercedes was a long way from new, but it was big and powerful and a pleasure to drive. It also had a full tank of fuel, and when she reached the roundabout on the outskirts of town she decided not to go back to her flat in London, where the press would undoubtedly be camped out and would be delighted by the picture she presented them with. It was not the way she intended to make the front page.

Besides, she had promised Gil that she would go home for James's birthday party. And she'd be safe there, safe from strangers in the dark and anything else that might threaten her.

So she pulled the disguising towel from her head, shook her hair free and took the road to the south coast.

Matt stirred as the sound of the shower brought him out of sleep for the second time. This time he stayed awake, rolled over onto his back and crooked his arms behind his head. He knew he was grinning from ear to ear but he couldn't help it. Last night he'd behaved himself, done the right thing. He deserved a reward for that. And that shower had been running for more than five minutes.

For a moment he pleasurably tortured himself with an image of the water sluicing over Nyssa's pale skin. With thoughts of what he might do to her, what she might do to him. All the fantasies he'd beaten back last night. Then he succumbed to temptation, throwing back the sheets and crossing to the bathroom.

The door was not quite shut, and he tapped on it and pushed it open a little further. The shower curtain was drawn along the bath, the room was full of steam, but it was nothing to the way he was steaming up inside.

'How do you feel about some company in there?' he called.

Teasingly, she didn't answer.

Well, he could tease too, as she would soon find out. 'Here I come, ready or not,' he called, and, closing the bathroom door behind him, he opened the shower cubicle.

It took a moment for the reality to sink in. Then the ten-foot-tall feeling dissipated like snow in August and he stood there, enveloped in steam, cursing his own stupidity with a fluency that would have raised even Nyssa's eyebrows.

He showered and reached for a towel. There was one. It was about the size of a postage stamp, which answered any question he might have about how she had managed to get away without causing a riot in Reception when she went to collect her room key.

He dried as best he could, shaved, dressed, packed his bag. And then, having gathered her clothes, he picked up the telephone and asked Reception to put him through to Nyssa's room.

'Miss Blake isn't in, sir.'

Of course she wasn't. She wouldn't have played charades with the shower if she'd been going back to her own room. There wouldn't have been any point because she must have realised he would go after her.

He dropped her clothes onto the bed. 'Did she check out, or are you expecting her back?'

There was a discreet clearing of the throat from the other end of the telephone, a pause.

'We're not quite sure of her movements, sir, but her car is still in the forecourt.'

'Then how—?' Instinctively, he slapped the pocket of his jacket and knew how. And to make matters worse he knew that if this had happened to anyone else he would be laughing. Just the way she was laughing at him.

Nyssa was hungry. She'd had no supper and no breakfast, and when she spotted a lay-by she pulled over to check the glove box. A torch, dark glasses, a packet of chocolate biscuits. Matt Crosby apparently had a weakness for the things. Or maybe he was perpetually prepared against the likelihood of missed meals.

Well, journalists lived to an uncertain schedule, she thought, taking one and munching it slowly. And she did want him to be a journalist. But there were other jobs where a man might not know when he was next going to eat, not all of them so... She grinned suddenly. 'Innocent' was the word that had come bubbling into her mind. It was not a word that

suited Matt Crosby, despite the way he'd behaved the previous night.

He'd been noble.

Not many red-blooded males would have
resisted the temptation she had flung in his
path.

But the way he'd kissed her had been anything but innocent.

She dragged her mind back from the mine-
field of exactly what Matt Crosby was, might
be. There was a telephone in the car. It was
time to stop daydreaming and get back to reality. And first she needed to call the
Delvering Arms and explain her precipitate
departure. The last thing she needed was bad
feeling in the town. After last night's fiasco
there would be enough of that. She picked up
the handset, turned it on and called the hotel.

'Good morning. The Delvering Arms,
Laura speaking, how may I help you?'

'Hi, Laura. This is Nyssa Blake. Could I
speak to the duty manager, please?'

'Yes, Miss Blake. Oh, Mr Crosby was looking for you. He left a message.' Well, what a

surprise. 'Would you like me to read it to you?'

'It might not be very polite,' Nyssa warned.

Laura giggled. 'It just says, ''I'll be in touch. Matt.'''

Remarkably restrained under the circumstances, but then what else could he say that wouldn't require the judicious use of the asterisk? 'Is that all? No telephone number?'

'That's all.' There was something slightly unnerving about that kind of self-control. You just knew there was going to be an explosion sooner or later. But you had no idea where or when. 'I expect he'll call you about your car.'

Her car?

'My car?'

'Mr Crosby said you lost your keys last night...'

'I did.'

'Well, he must have found them, because he left in it about ten minutes ago.'

'Oh.' What had he done? Jump-started it? And if he had? What kind of man did that make him? Resourceful? Well, he'd already demonstrated that. 'Er, good.'

Nyssa spoke briefly to the manager, then started the car. About to slide it into gear, she decided it might be a good idea to turn off the telephone. It had nothing whatever to do with the possibility of Matt deciding to call her and give her a piece of his mind, she told herself, simply a safety precaution. Everyone knew how dangerous it was to drive and talk on the telephone at the same.

The soft burble of the phone cut into her reasoning. She'd left it too late. Of course she could simply turn it off. But then he would know she was there and he would think she was a coward. She couldn't bear that.

The phone rang again and she picked it up. 'Nyssa Blake,' she said, in her best rounded vowels.

'Good morning, Nyssa Blake.'

'Matt?' Damn. His name had been startled from her, even though she had known it would be him. And if *she* could hear the shake in her voice, so could he.

'You were expecting a call from someone else?'

'No…no.' She just hadn't anticipated his voice, softly threatening, to make her tremble quite like that. 'Look, I'm sorry about the car—' she began. He wasn't listening.

'I was really looking forward to joining you in the shower this morning. I was lying there, listening to it running and thinking of all the really wicked things I was going to do to you to make up for my restraint last night,' he said. There was a low, sensuous growl somewhere deep in his throat that told her he meant it. Really meant it. 'That was a shocking waste of water. You should be ashamed of yourself.' She was! She really was! But it had been a question of self-preservation. 'Where are you, Nyssa?'

'Matt—' she began.

'Or, more to the point, where's my car?'

She had been about to tell him. The heat in his voice had sizzled down the phone, burning her up, and she had been about to say, I'm here, parked in a lay-by on the A whatever-it-was. Come and get me. The fact that she would have meant it was seriously worrying. But apparently there was no need to worry, because all that heavy breathing had simply been for effect. The only thing he was interested in right now was his wretched Mercedes.

'What's your problem, Matt? You're not short of transport, are you? I understood from the receptionist at the Delvering Arms that you had made other arrangements.'

'Temporary arrangements. This tin can of yours is not my idea of a quality motoring experience.'

'It's very economical,' she pointed out.

'What it is, my dear, is very small, very noisy and very slow. And the fuel gauge is on empty. I have to tell you that I am not at all happy with the exchange.'

'You wouldn't consider it on a permanent basis, then?'

'No.'

'That's a pity. Your car is an absolute dream to drive. No complaints at all.'

'Where the hell are you?' he demanded. The hot gravel had gone. He was just plain angry.

'Do you want a four-figure map reference?'

'You know what I want.'

The growl was back, but she refused to be fooled a second time. 'Somewhere between A and B,' she said sharply. 'A is, of course, Delvering. Well, you could work that out for yourself. And, if you've done your homework thoroughly, you'll know the location of B.'

'Nyssa!'

'If you can find me, Matt, I'll let you read me the Riot Act about wasting water. Maybe we could waste a little more—'

Whoa!

'Nyssa—' His voice was shaking now.

Nyssa dropped the phone onto the handset and switched it off before he could call back, then slumped back against the soft leather upholstery with a groan.

What on earth had made her do that? Had she quite lost her head? Didn't she have enough on her mind without inviting Matt to indulge in an idiotic game of cat-and-mouse?

Suppose he caught her?

She tucked the towel more firmly around her waist, wrapped his shirt protectively about her. That was a mistake too. It was impregnated with his scent. But she didn't take it off. She just slipped Matt's lovely car into gear and drove away.

CHAPTER FOUR

NYSSA drove the Mercedes around to the back of her stepfather's imposing Georgian mansion. She hoped to slip in through the back door and up to the top-floor 'daughter' flat without being seen.

She'd been given the key when Sophia and James had married and, although she spent very little time there, she was grateful for the chance to be private and gather her thoughts before facing her mother.

It was not to be. She ran lightly up the back stairs and had just reached the first floor when her mother emerged from her bedroom. Sophia Lambert's silver-blonde hair was curved into an immaculate pageboy style, her slender figure draped elegantly in a pair of softly pleated grey linen trousers, a wickedly expensive silk shirt. She was busy fastening gold clips to her ears and for a moment didn't spot her daughter. But Nyssa knew there was no escape.

'Hello, Sophia.'

Her mother's head turned in her direction and for a moment she seemed riveted to the spot. Then, 'Nyssa, darling, we were so worried about you,' she said, stretching out her arms in greeting. 'What happened? Where on earth have you been?' Having hugged her daughter, she held her shoulders and stood back, regarding her unconventional travelling clothes from beneath a pair of finely arched brows. 'Or is it indiscreet to ask?'

'I take it from all this motherly concern that we made the ten o'clock news?' Nyssa had tried, really tried, to come to terms with her widowed mother's marriage to James Lambert.

'Did you doubt it?' She heard the sigh in her mother's voice and longed, somewhere deep inside, to reach out and hug her the way she'd used to. But always between them lay the grave in the little country churchyard up on the Downs where her father lay. That bitter sense of betrayal. Her father had been a hero while James Lambert was a property developer. All right, he wasn't like Parker, all quick profit and no added value. But still. 'You really might have thought of ringing to let us know you were safe. No one seemed to know where you were. I rang the hotel, but they said you hadn't come back.'

'Actually, I was there. I took the back way in to avoid reporters and spent the night hiding out—' She flipped the corner of the towel she was wearing as a skirt and managed a grin. 'In the linen cupboard.'

'Really? How enterprising. On your own, or did you share it with the owner of the shirt?'

'Oh, we shared,' she said carelessly. Then found herself blushing. 'He's my self-appointed minder.'

'Is that what they're calling it these days?' Sophia smiled as she put a gentle hand on her daughter's arm. 'Why don't you take a shower and then come and have some lunch with us? You must be starving.' About to decline on automatic, Nyssa heard her stomach rebel noisily and Sophia laughed. 'Was that a yes?'

'Well... Now you mention it I haven't had anything but a chocolate biscuit since some time yesterday.'

'That's the trouble with linen cupboards. No Room Service. It'll be ready in about twenty minutes.' She turned away, then hesitated and looked back. 'It's lovely to have you home, Nyssa. We see so little of you.' Then, as she passed a window, 'Have you got a new car? What happened to the pram on wheels?' She turned anxiously. 'You haven't had an accident?'

'No, nothing like that. I had to make a quick getaway from Delvering, and as I lost my keys in the scuffle in the Assembly Room I borrowed that one.'

'It's a bit of a brute. I always think those big Mercs are more of a man's car.'

'You're right. And if the man who owns it is half as bright as I think he is, it won't be long before he comes looking for it.' She flipped her brows. 'And his shirt. You see, I didn't actually ask him before I borrowed them.'

Sophia Lambert raised her own brows the barest fraction in response. 'You have been having an interesting time. Will he be very cross?'

Cross? That wasn't a word that quite matched Matt Crosby. Altogether too wishy-washy... Then she realised her mother was still waiting for an answer.

'The words ''wet'' and ''hen'' leap to mind,' she confessed.

Sophia laughed. 'You don't seem particularly worried about it.'

'To be honest, the angrier he is the better I'll like it.' If he were too nice she'd know he was a fake.

'More and more interesting. I confess I can hardly wait to meet him. I take it you are expecting him to turn up some time during the weekend?'

Nyssa gave another tiny shrug, unwilling to betray just how much she was hoping he would turn up, angry or not.

'Blame Gil. He said it was about time I brought someone home. I wouldn't want to disappoint you by bringing someone boringly conventional.'

Sophia Lambert's smile was a touch rueful. 'I think we can rely on you not to disappoint us in that direction, darling.'

He didn't turn up for lunch. Well, what had she expected? That he would come racing after her, *ventre à terre*, like some lovelorn swain? The idea was patently ridiculous.

But he would want his car back. And he'd want his story. Correction. She'd handed him a story on a plate. Would he be able to resist it? It would be a story the tabloids would love and would probably pay well for, but would Matt Crosby be angry enough to write it?

If he did it would give her the answer to one question. It was what a freelance journalist would do.

And if he didn't? What did that make him?

Suspect? Or clever? Or just kind? Or any combination she might care to choose.

In the meantime, she reminded herself, she had more to worry about than one man and his car. She picked up the phone and called Sky.

'Nyssa! For heaven's sake, what happened to you? We've all been worried sick. And I've been plagued by reporters all morning.'

She buried the rush of guilt in irony. 'Really? I'd have thought they'd have got enough news and photographs last night to fill their newspapers.'

'All right, maybe I exaggerated. One reporter. But a tall, dark and distinctly dishy one, if you like that well-lived-in look...which I do.' Matt Crosby. The guilt evaporated in a cloud of euphoria. 'I thought I'd got him hooked last night, but, as always, once he'd seen you no one else would do.' Sky laughed, but didn't quite manage to disguise the edge in her voice. 'Maybe if I coloured my hair red I'd get some attention.'

'You're welcome. It's wildly overrated.'

'I'd like the opportunity to find that out for myself. Now, to business.'

*   *   *

'I don't know what you're talking about, Crosby.' Parker briefly glanced at the cheque Matt had tossed onto his desk then stared up at him with disbelief. Maybe no one had ever flung his money back at him before.

Matt knew his mistake had been to take it in the first place. But principles did not come cheap and the rent still had to be paid. 'You expect me to believe that?'

'Believe it not; it doesn't bother me. But I didn't organise the break-up of Nyssa Blake's little party for the press. It wouldn't have made sense.' Parker leaned back in his chair. 'I do have to admit, though, that I did rather enjoy seeing the tables turned. How did she like having her plans upset for a change?'

Matt refused to be sidetracked. 'What about kidnapping?' he demanded. 'Would that have made sense?'

'Kidnapping?' He laughed. 'Tell me, Crosby, did you take a crack on the skull in that skirmish?'

Matt, infuriated by the man's continued pretence, reached across the desk and, grabbing hold of the lapels of his expensive Italian suit, lifted him clear out of his chair. 'Answer my question,' he demanded, with quiet insistence.

Charles Parker's mouth abruptly stopped smiling. Instead it opened and then closed again in a pretty fair impersonation of a goldfish. Then he blinked nervously and said, 'What kidnapping?'

'Innocence doesn't suit you, Parker. But if the lady gets hurt, I promise you I'll be back.' Then, disgusted with himself for ever getting involved, he dropped the man back into his chair and turned to leave.

'Crosby!' Matt didn't stop, but strode across the acres of ankle-deep carpet towards the door. 'Crosby, wait. Please.' The 'please' had practically choked him. 'What kidnapping?' he repeated.

'You tell me. You were the one who wanted Nyssa Blake locked away in some deep, dark dungeon.'

'In my dreams.' Then, 'For heaven's sake man, if the girl is missing I'm not going to weep crocodile tears, but I'm hardly about to jump for joy either. Don't you think I'm the first person everyone will suspect? Has she been kidnapped?'

'No. But not for want of trying.'

Parker had been smoothing out his rumpled silk tie, but something in Matt's voice caught his attention. 'Good God, you rescued her, didn't you?' And he laughed. 'Priceless. You deserve a bonus for that alone. You've saved me no end of trouble.' For the first time, doubt entered Matt Crosby's mind. 'Tell me, Crosby, does she know that you're working for me?'

'I'm not. You've got your money back, although you don't deserve it. I told you, Parker, no dirty business.'

'And I heard you. I want the lady stopped, but I'm well aware that violence is not the answer. If it were I wouldn't need to pay for your kind of help.' He sat back down in his oversized chair and indicated the one in front of his desk. 'Come and sit down, man.'

Matt retraced his steps, but didn't take the chair. 'Are you absolutely sure that everyone who works for you understands your point of view?' he asked. 'Isn't there just a possibility that you might have muttered something along the lines of—Who will rid me of this troublesome female?'

'I can see where you're headed, but, no, I don't want anything bad to happen to Miss Blake. It's her reputation that I want to see in shreds.'

'Well, someone grabbed Nyssa last night when the lights went out and I can assure you that he wasn't asking her to dance.'

Parker was thoughtful. 'You seem to be taking this rather personally, Crosby. Was she very grateful?'

It took all Matt Crosby's self-control not to hit the man. Protecting Nyssa Blake was getting to be a habit. A bad habit. She was quite capable of taking care of herself. If the casual manner in which she'd hijacked his car was not enough to convince him, the bruises on his shin were developing like an out-of-focus

Polaroid. 'I don't like men who frighten women,' he said, refusing to rise to Parker's bait.

Parker made a dismissive gesture, as if the whole idea was really too ridiculous to contemplate. 'No one who works for me would be that stupid. And neither should you be.' He had obviously recovered from his shaking. 'You've got enough money troubles without throwing the stuff away, so if you've quite finished bawling me out for something I didn't do I suggest you pick up that cheque and get on with the job I'm paying you for, before I change my mind.'

'Keep your money,' Matt said, turning to leave. 'I've already changed mine.'

'I think you're making a mistake, Mr Crosby.'

Matt grasped the handle of the door, unimpressed by his sudden elevation to misterhood. 'The only mistake I made was in taking this job in the first place. I'm not that desperate.'

'But you're angry. It's clouding your judgement.' Matt Crosby didn't need Parker to tell him that. His judgement had flown out of the window the moment he had set eyes on Nyssa Blake. Held her in his arms. Being made a fool of, then driving fifty miles in her rattle-bucket of a car hadn't done a great deal for his temper, either. When he caught up with her... When he caught up with her they would exchange car keys and he would walk away. End of story. 'Think for a moment,' Parker said, just a touch desperately.

'Well?' Matt demanded irritably. 'What is it?'

'Simply this. If I didn't order the meeting broken up last night, and Miss Blake carried off who knows where, then you have to ask yourself one question...' And quite suddenly Parker had got all of Matt Crosby's attention. 'Who did?'

His eyes narrowed. In truth he hadn't given the matter any thought because Parker had been his only suspect. Was still top of the list, despite his denials. But nevertheless the man had a point.

He shrugged. 'Supposing I believe you? What then?'

'Supposing you do, Mr Crosby. I've spent a lot of money on public relations, and now someone is going out of his way to make me appear in a less than sympathetic light.'

'That's not exactly difficult.'

'No, it's become unfashionable to provide people with the built environment they want and need, which is why you won't be the only one to jump to all the wrong conclusions about last night.'

'My heart bleeds for you.'

'I'm glad to hear it, because I'd like to know who's behind it, Crosby. And something tells me that with your new-found concern for the lady's safety you're just the man to find out.' He sat back in his huge black leather chair. 'It might even be Miss Blake herself,' he added, as an afterthought. 'She, after all, would have the most to gain from making me appear a black-hearted villain.'

Matt swallowed the obvious retort and said, 'That's ridiculous.'

'Is it?'

No, it wasn't. Not really. Except he didn't think that Nyssa would stoop to such deceit…which just went to prove how badly she had affected his judgement. His own situation provided ample evidence of precisely how low people would stoop…

'If you're so sure about that, Mr Crosby, why don't you come down off that high horse of yours long enough to convince me?' He pushed the cheque towards him.

Tempting as it was to snatch it back, Matt kept his distance. He'd do the job, but not for Parker. This was personal. 'Keep your money, Parker. I'm working for myself on this one.'

'Whatever you say.' He glanced at the cheque in his hand before folding it and placing it in his jacket pocket. 'In the meantime, if you find out anything, let me know.' He patted his jacket. 'I'll be happy to let you have this back any time.'

*   *   *

'Did anyone ring for me?'

Nyssa had been persuaded to go shopping for a dress for the party with her mother, but the moment she returned she'd sought out James.

'There's a list by the phone,' he told her. She grabbed it. There were a dozen names but Matt Crosby's name wasn't among them. James, watching her, clearly picked up her disappointment. 'Why don't you call him?' he suggested, kindly. 'Invite him to the party.'

'No. It doesn't matter.' It wasn't true. It mattered like hell. It shouldn't, but it did. 'But I would like to use the telephone. '

'Help yourself,' he said, making a move to rise as she punched in a number.

'Don't go, James. It isn't anything private. Sky? Can you do something for me?' She hadn't told Sky about the attempted kidnapping. She wasn't ready to talk about what had happened just yet and certainly not on a cellphone, where any interested snoop with a radio receiver could be listening in. 'Have you got a number for Matt Crosby?'

'I have.'

'Give him a call, will you? Tell him that his car will be in the car park at the Delvering Arms on Monday morning.'

'His car?' She could almost hear Sky straining not to ask the obvious question. 'That's all?'

'That's all,' she confirmed. 'No, wait. Did you happen to find my handbag when you were clearing up at the Assembly Rooms?'

'Sorry. Was there anything important in it?'

'Nothing much. Just my car keys.' *Aaah.* 'Tell me, Sky, did Mr Crosby go into the main hall at the Assembly Rooms when he called round the morning after the meeting?'

'Just to look for his notebook. Is it important?'

'Everything is important, Sky. Ask around, will you? See if anyone knows him. In fact you'd better run a check on everyone who came to the meeting.'

While she tried to remember exactly what was in her bag.

*   *   *

Matt sat with the little bag on his desk. From his earliest days he'd known that a woman's handbag was sacrosanct, private, not to be touched.

Okay, so he'd taken her car keys, but this was different. He'd search computer records, files, even desk drawers when the opportunity arose without turning a hair, but handbags always made him feel just a bit queasy.

But she'd challenged him to find her. He had her London address and telephone number; they were in the file that Parker had given him. He'd gone there after his confrontation with the man, but there had been no one home.

He'd tried the phone later and continued to call at regular intervals until midnight. It had rung unanswered. There wasn't even a machine to take a message. London was not point B. He wasn't even sure he wanted to find point B. Not until he'd taken a little time to decide exactly what he was going to do when he got there.

Of course, if he took the shower she'd promised him, that wouldn't be a problem.

In order to distract himself, he picked up her bag. It was small, made of soft, expensive black leather. It wouldn't hold much. None of the clutter that everyday bags accumulated— the bills, till receipts from the supermarket, letters; the mundane items that gave away so much information. He just hoped there would be enough to make up for the nasty taste that going through it would leave in his mouth.

He opened it and tipped out the contents. A comb, a lipstick, a white handkerchief edged with lace. A pen. A little appointment diary.

He picked up the diary. Inside was her name, her smart London address and telephone number. It gave her mother's name as the person to contact in case of emergency. A Sussex telephone number and address. Point B? One of the cellphones on the desk beside him rang. The one he'd bought for the Parker enquiry. He'd only given two people that number. Parker was one. He hoped it wasn't him.

'Matt Crosby,' he said.

'Hi, Matt. This is Sky.'

'The lady I still owe a drink.'

'The very same. Nyssa asked me to tell you that she'd leave your car on the forecourt of the Delvering Arms on Monday morning.' She waited, hoping for some explanation. When it wasn't forthcoming, she said, 'You can pay your debts then, if you like?'

'My pleasure.'

Monday? That suggested Nyssa was in no hurry to return his car. But the fact that she'd had Sky ring, remind him that he was supposed to be looking for her, hinted otherwise, and he smiled as he picked up the diary, dialled the Sussex number.

'Broomhill six thousand.'

Nyssa was a hundred miles away, but that low, husky voice still turned him inside out, made him feel that she was right there in the room, beside him. The sound evoked her hot eyes, the creamy skin of her neck, the smooth rise of her breasts as her dress had hit the floor.

'And would that be Point B?' he enquired, his own voice thick with desire.

There was the tiniest hesitation before she replied. 'You've taken your time, Mr Crosby, considering you stole my handbag.'

'I rescued it, Nyssa. Kept it safe. Just like I rescued you.'

'But you didn't rush to return it. Instead you took my car keys, and, since you've found me, you must have read my diary, as well. Not the act of a gentleman.'

'I thought we'd already decided that, since I'm a journalist, I couldn't possibly be a gentleman.' He thought he heard a muffled laugh, and he couldn't stop himself from smiling as he added, 'Don't worry, your secrets are safe with me.'

'What secrets?' she came back sharply. 'There wasn't anything... Oh, sure, very funny.' She cleared her throat. 'Did Sky ring you? About exchanging cars?'

He didn't think she wanted to exchange cars in front of the Delvering Arms and then walk away. The words were right, but the voice she was saying them with was sending an entirely contrary message.

'On Monday?' she said, when he didn't immediately answer.

'I don't think I can wait that long, Nyssa. Besides, it isn't quite what we agreed.'

'Agreed?'

'If I found you.'

Nyssa hung up, cutting him off. Her mother, arranging flowers on the kitchen table, turned and stared. 'Is something the matter, darling?'

'No,' she said quickly. 'Nothing.' She sank into the nearest chair, pulling at the neck of her T-shirt. Flapping the air with her hand. 'Is it hot, or is it just me?'

Sophia Lambert raised her brows slightly. 'I'd say it was whoever was on the other end of the telephone just now. Try a cold shower.'

Matt grinned. Hanging up on him was a good sign. It meant that she remembered promising to indulge in a little water conservation with him. For a moment he indulged himself in the fantasy of sharing a shower with Nyssa Blake.

Then he dragged himself back to the task in hand, flicking through her appointments. It was crammed with the dates of council meetings, planning meetings. There was even an appointment with a senior official at the Department of the Environment. No wonder Parker was worried.

There were also the everyday things, like family birthdays, appointments at the hairdressers and the dentist, beside which she'd drawn a little face with a turned down mouth. He found himself smiling sympathetically.

Inside the back cover there was a small pocket, for stamps and suchlike. It contained a photograph of two men, their medal ribbons bright against their uniform jackets. One was recognisably Nyssa's father. The other was younger, taller. A heroic figure, the kind of man to turn a young girl's head. He turned it over, but there was nothing written on the back, nothing to say who he was.

Nothing to account for the unexpected heat of jealousy that burned in the pit of his stomach.

He replaced it and turned to the current week, reminding himself that he was doing this not for Parker, but for her. There were a number of appointments with journalists. One with Drew, Makepeace, a major firm of accountants. He made a note of that.

The presentation at the Assembly Rooms was listed for yesterday. Nothing for today. Saturday—James's birthday. James? That had to be James Lambert. Her stepfather. He picked up his phone and called the financial journalist, an old friend, who'd organised his press pass and invitation to Nyssa's presentation.

'Terry? Matt Crosby.' They exchanged pleasantries, touching on the skirmish at Delvering before Matt got to the point. 'Can you tell me what kind of party there's going to be for James Lambert's birthday this weekend?'

He returned with the information that there was going to be a seriously large thrash at the man's Sussex mansion. Family, friends, major players from the business world.

'Black tie?'

Terry groaned. 'You're not planning on gatecrashing, are you? I should warn you that the guest list includes some people who really, really don't like you.'

'That's a long list. You'd be surprised how few people want to be seen with a man who goes from a triple A credit rating to the top of everyone's black list overnight.'

'It's nothing to do with the credit rating. You just know too much. Spill the beans and I could make all your wildest dreams come true.'

'I very much doubt that.' His dreams had recently taken a diversion. They no longer concentrated on seeing the directors of a large merchant bank hounded from the City and instead involved a girl with red hair, blue eyes and legs that were pure sin. 'Your legal people would never sanction it without cast-iron proof.'

'When you've got it, call me.'

'Sure.' In the meantime it was time he found out exactly why Nyssa had been to see Drew, Makepeace. He opened his laptop and set to work.

It was late before he finished. It hadn't been easy, but it hadn't been nearly difficult enough to find exactly the kind of information Charles Parker had been hoping he'd dig up. He'd wanted to know how Nyssa financed her activities and he'd pay well to discover that most of the money came through her mother, from shares invested by her father in one of the construction companies she'd campaigned against so vigorously.

That was information to tarnish her bright image.

He wondered if she knew. Probably not. It wouldn't matter anyway. Her enemies would have a field-day with such revelations, conveniently ignoring the charity she'd just registered to raise funds to restore the Gaumont to its former glory. Heroes—and heroines— were raised up only to be knocked down. They'd make a laughing stock of her.

Not if he could help it. Which was why he rang Parker at home to let him know that he'd thought it over, and was back on the job, hot on the trail, buying himself a little time to figure out what to do.

CHAPTER FIVE

'Wow! That dress is sensational,' Kitty greeted her warmly. 'Give me a twirl.'

Nyssa obliged and the dress, a delicate spiral of midnight-blue silk chiffon edged with silver thread, wound from one shoulder to a point some way short of her knees, floated lightly around her as she spun on a pair of high-heeled strappy sandals.

'It's absolutely perfect.' And she patted her bump, very noticeable despite the softly muted shades of the crushed silk gown that flowed loosely from her shoulders to the floor. 'Believe it or not I once used to wear dresses that short.'

'Gil told me about the baby. Congratulations.'

'Poor Gil, he's blaming himself for not staying with you.'

'I don't need a bodyguard,' Nyssa replied quickly. 'It was nothing.' Of course if Matt hadn't been there it might have been very different. 'Gil clearly has other things to keep him busy.' And she waggled her eyebrows suggestively.

Her stepsister grinned. 'I promise you it beats the hell out of living in a tree on long winter nights.'

Once, just once, Nyssa had been on a demonstration that involved spending a night in a tree and she'd never been allowed to forget it. Usually she jumped on to the defensive, but this time she just grinned and rather enjoyed the look of surprise that flashed across Kitty's face as she said, 'That rather depends on who's sharing your tree.'

'What an interesting life you do lead, Nyssa.'

'I certainly try.' Then, 'I'd better circulate for a while.' Nyssa moved away, stopping to chat to family friends and people who had seen the news and wanted to know what had happened at Delvering. She played down the disruption, assuring everyone that such an early attack was a good sign, demonstrating that the opposition was severely rattled. The attempted kidnap she kept to herself.

But the fact that Matt hadn't turned up on her doorstep, or at least telephoned, still niggled at her. Maybe she should be relieved. At a distance she didn't have to worry whether he was using her, or she was using him. Whether he was her friend or her enemy.

So why was she hanging around the front door? And why, each time she caught sight of a dark head, a tall, broad-shouldered figure approaching the entrance, did her nerves flutter treacherously, her skin tingle with anticipation? What caused that ridiculous dip of disappointment when she saw that it wasn't him?

She was beginning to wish she had taken Gil's advice and invited someone—anyone. Pete even.

Then she caught her mother watching her and, cross with herself for being so obvious, she took a glass of champagne from a passing tray and headed out through the open drawing room windows and along the canopied walk to a marquee where there was a small band playing.

Already the dance floor was crowded and she saw Gil and Kitty wrapped in each other's arms, moving slowly in time to something smoochy being belted out on a saxophone. Gil could find out all about Matt, she thought. More than she wanted to know, in all probability.

There had been a time when she'd have used any excuse to speak to Gil. But this was a party. Not the moment. Or maybe she wasn't in a big hurry to get bad news.

She turned away, restless and edgy, taking a sip of champagne in the hopes that it might lend her just a hint of its sparkle. But it was going to take more than champagne, she realised, and abandoned the glass, and the loud marquee, and took herself into the scented darkness of the garden.

As Matt Crosby drove through James Lambert's tall wrought-iron gates he wondered if he had made a mistake. Maybe he should have phoned Nyssa first after all. She was probably deeply embarrassed at the way she'd sobbed herself to sleep in his arms. At waking up in bed with him hours later.

Maybe he should drive her car around to the rear of the house and leave it, with the keys in the glove compartment, and save them both an awkward few minutes. With any luck he'd find his own car; he'd brought a spare set of keys with him so he could simply drive it away.

She would know that he had found her. The ball would be firmly in her court. But suppose she didn't lob it back, refused even to give him an interview? Always supposing she had ever believed that he was a journalist.

He couldn't risk that. He had to find out who had ordered that near-riot to cover an attempt at kidnapping. Disturbingly he had a feeling that it might be a whole lot easier to answer that one than work out why he cared. Or why Nyssa had taken off like a scared rabbit at the crack of dawn.

If she'd wanted to leave he wouldn't have stopped her; she hadn't had to creep out like that. Then a cold finger traced his spine. Was that it? Did she think he would have stopped her? Did she think, after all, that he might be part of what had happened? A new take on the bad guy/good guy routine.

An expletive hissed through his teeth and he swung out of the car and strode down the drive. He wouldn't do anything to hurt her, and he was determined to put her straight about that before he went anywhere.

Except, of course, that was why he had been in Delvering. Not to cause her physical pain. But to uncover her secrets. Find some way to blacken her name.

He came to an abrupt halt in the open doorway. Too late. He'd already been spotted by a silver-blonde. She immediately excused herself from the group she was with and headed towards him. He'd have known she was Nyssa's mother even if he hadn't seen her photograph in Parker's file.

'Matt Crosby,' he said, immediately introducing himself. 'I'm afraid I'm gatecrashing your party, Mrs Lambert.'

'Are you? Shall I fetch someone to throw you out?' she enquired, but since she was smiling he assumed she wasn't serious.

'I'll go quietly, I promise. I just wanted a word with Nyssa. I've brought her car back.'

'Tell me, Mr Crosby,' she said, after a moment, 'just what linen cupboard did my daughter find you in? And are there any more at home like you?'

Matt knew that if he had been capable of blushing he would have done exactly that. Instead he just about managed a smile. 'Matt,' he said, rather stupidly. 'And, no, Mrs Lambert. There's just me. My mother said I was more than enough.'

'She's wrong. The world can never have too many reckless men.'

He thought it wiser to decline the obvious invitation to explore that remark, and glanced around. 'Is Nyssa here? I don't want to be a nuisance, but I was hoping to retrieve my car—'

'And the dinner jacket was the first thing that came to hand when you opened the wardrobe?' Sophia Lambert enquired, then laughed. 'At least stay and have a drink, meet the rest of the family.' She handed him a glass of champagne and took another herself. 'It was clever of you to make Nyssa wait. She's been like a cat on a hot brick waiting for you to turn up and give her what she deserves for running off with your lovely car.'

He wasn't entirely sure where this conversation was heading, but he had the feeling it would be easy to like Sophia Lambert. 'And what is that?'

She laughed again. 'You're cool, Matt Crosby. Reckless, clever and cool. I don't know whether to envy my daughter or pity her.' She touched the arm of a man standing with his back to them. 'Gil, this is Nyssa's friend, Matt Crosby. My son-in-law, Gil Paton. Gil, darling, will you take care of Matt for me?' she said as people continued to arrive, pushing them further into the house. 'Have another drink,' she said, taking Matt's empty glass and putting a full one in his hand.

'Thanks, but I'm driving.'

'Don't. Stay over. We're having a beach party tomorrow—' Someone greeted her with a squeal of excitement. 'I'm sure we can find you a spare linen cupboard,' she called, as she was swept away.

Gil Paton. The man Nyssa had assumed he was working for. The young hero in the photograph with Nyssa's father, older now by ten or more years. And married to Nyssa's stepsister. What the hell did that mean?

'Good to meet you,' Paton said, extending his hand in welcome. 'I'm glad Nyssa invited someone down for the weekend.'

He sounded genuine enough, even perhaps a little relieved. Did he know about the photograph? Or just suspect that he was the object of hero-worship? A pedestal could be a mighty uncomfortable perch.

'Actually, she didn't—'

'Look, just follow the noise,' he said, waving through the open doors as someone else demanded his attention. 'She was in the marquee…you'll find her sooner or later.'

Matt didn't doubt it. Of course she might tell him to get lost, in which case he'd just have to try and forget the searing memory of her skin, pale and translucent as alabaster against the vivid heat of her hair…

It wouldn't be easy, he thought, as he stood in the entrance to the marquee and looked around. There were a lot of people dancing, sitting at the small tables drinking, talking, but there was no flash of bright hair to tempt him to join them.

He wasn't attracted to the crush and sensed that she would hate it too. Out there, in the shadowy dark of the late summer garden, was where he would find her.

The air was heavy with the scent of roses, and as he brushed against an archway that led beyond the formal gardens to a small orchard beyond Matt was showered with velvety petals.

He was tempted to pick one of the flowers and go courting his lady beneath the heavily laden fruit trees. But it was a ridiculous fantasy and one he found easy to resist. Before he offered the lady flowers, he'd make sure of his welcome.

Nyssa, sitting on an old weather-silvered garden seat, had thought she was safe from all interruption. She had appeared at the party, done her duty. After a while she would take another turn around the crowded marquee, smile and dance a little, be polite to people she scarcely knew and didn't much want to.

For now she was content to sit back and listen to the tiny night sounds, watch the bats flitter through the trees as they chased moths. That was until she heard the rustle of leaves as someone brushed against the rose arch. Then it all came rushing back. That moment in the Assembly Rooms at Delvering, that moment when a man's hand clamped over her mouth, when his arm grabbed her around the waist and lifted her from her feet.

Out in the woods she would have heard the sound much sooner, but here, with the faint background thumping of the band, the rise and fall of distant voices, she had missed it, and now it was her heart that was thumping, fear drying her mouth as she shrank back into the darkness. Then she heard her name being called, very softly.

'Nyssa?'

Matt! He'd come! The eager heartleap left her in no doubt how she felt about his unannounced arrival. As the air stilled expectantly it took every ounce of will-power to hold back from launching herself at him, flinging herself into his arms.

But she balled her hands into fists and bit back an eager cry. She had run from him because she didn't trust him. She had no reason to change her mind about that and she kept very still, waiting for him to leave, willing him to walk away.

Yet she hugged the knowledge that he had come. It was a new feeling, to have someone want her. Whatever else he might be faking, she was sure he hadn't been faking that.

Matt waited. He was certain she was there, somewhere beneath the trees. Was she hiding because she was afraid of him? Or was this just a teasing game?

Nyssa, listening hard, heard the telltale squeak of damp grass against leather soles. He wasn't leaving; he was a step nearer. Her skin prickled with the knowledge, her breasts gorged with excitement, a sweet heaviness low in her abdomen invaded her entire being. Was it always like this?

Matt caught her scent. Floral and yet utterly different from the roses. Greener, but heavy and sensual. It should have been wrong for a woman like Nyssa, but it wasn't.

It was quite dark now. The night had closed around them in the orchard. But, guided by the scent, he became surer. He stopped within feet of her, knew that he could put out his hand and touch her. But he didn't. He leaned against the gnarled trunk of an old tree and said, 'I've brought your car back.'

Nyssa was practically shaking. She had been expecting him to touch her. Reach out for her. Hold her as he had in Delvering. The cool voice came as a shock. He was still angry with her. He had every right to be angry. Well, if he'd come looking for an apology he would wait a long time.

'You took your time about it,' she said, as if she'd been sitting there waiting for him to turn up.

He heard the nervous snatch at her throat, the faint tremor in her voice. The words were casual, but a little too sharp. Beneath the confident, in-your-face manner, he suspected she was shaking.

Well, that made two of them. His pulse was hammering at his throat and it was as if his skin was a size too small for him. Her scent had been a part of him for every waking moment of the last two days, and now he was standing beside her in the dark, so close that he could reach out and touch her. In his mind he could feel the silken white shoulder of her skin, her hair against his cheek, his mouth at her throat.

This was new. The urgency stretching his self-control to breaking point. The certainty that he must wait. First he had to win her trust. Once he had that, anything was possible.

He tightened his fingers, curling them into his palm. 'I told you, I've been busy,' he said. 'May I sit down?' He sensed rather than saw her shrug.

'Did you bring my handbag as well as my car?' she demanded as he joined her on the bench.

'I needed transport, Nyssa. I had to have your keys.'

'Really?' She turned to him, her face pale against the night. 'And there was me imagining you jump-starting it like some movie bad guy—'

'That was Plan B,' he said, cutting her off before she got too near the truth. 'Keys are tidier.'

'Well, I'll get yours and then you can go—'

Nyssa made a move to stand, but he caught her hand in his and as she sank back onto the seat she reached with her other hand to feel for the swollen knuckles. 'How's your hand?'

'It's fine,' he said, the words thick in his throat as her fingers sought out the grazes. Absolutely perfect. 'I met some of your family. Your mother. Gil Paton.' Her heard her swallow nervously.

'Really? Did you like him?'

'Does it matter?' She didn't answer. 'You thought I was one of his men,' he reminded her. 'Does he always look out for you?'

'Not if I can stop him.'

'I think you might need him on this job.'

'No!' Then, 'I don't want him fussing around me.'

'Don't you? Then maybe it's time you got rid of the photograph.'

She turned on him. 'That's a bit low, isn't it, Matt? Even for a man capable of searching through a woman's handbag.'

He'd been doing a lot worse than that. But her safety was his prime concern and for that he was prepared to do anything. 'You challenged me to find you. And you did steal my car.'

'Rubbish! I borrowed it! You know I did.'

'I always thought borrowing involved a request that started with the word "please"'

'And if I'd asked, said pretty please, would you have said yes?'

'We'll never know, will we?' He stood up. 'But I'm prepared to forget it if you'll offer me something to eat. It's been a long time since lunch.'

'No chocolate biscuits?'

'Your car wasn't much of an exchange.'

'No. A food-free zone.' From the darkness came the hint of a giggle. 'I'm sorry, Matt. Of course you must stay and have some supper.'

'And a drink?'

'The champagne is flowing like… champagne,' she assured him. 'Anything else?'

'A dance would be nice. Something slow and not too demanding. It's been a tough week. I've got the bruises to show for it.'

'You'll have more if you dance with me,' she warned him.

'I'll take the risk,' he said, stretching out his hand to her. 'If you will.' And she took it and let him pull her up beside him.

'Supper, a drink and a dance,' she said, quickly. 'I owe you that much for taking the trouble to return my car.'

Before she could let go, he tightened his grip. 'I haven't finished,' he said.

'I have—'

'Not quite, sweetheart. Supper, a few dances, then afterwards…'

'Afterwards?' The word was startled from her.

'This.' And he pulled her swiftly into his arms, needing to know that he hadn't imagined the heat.

Nyssa was no stranger to the unexpected. Her life was lived on the edge and she was ready for it. But this was different. Dangerously different. Nothing in all her experience had prepared her for the surge of longing that bypassed all the warning signals, ignoring the lights on red as Matt's mouth descended like a brand to claim her.

Even as her mind scrambled to action, seeking to formulate some kind of resistance, he released her hand to cradle her face gently between his fingers, kissing her so thoroughly that coherent thought didn't stand a chance. And her lips parted, surrendered without so much as a token protest. Her mouth was too blissfully engaged on a journey of discovery to take time out to search for words like *stop…no…wait…*

He'd kissed her in Delvering. In Delvering she had been too shaken, too distraught for anything other than basic reaction. Given days in which to formulate a more studied approach, it seemed her reaction was pretty much the same. Very basic.

'That's not afterwards,' she said breathlessly, after what seemed like an eternity during which he had taken her on a ride that beat anything in the amusement park at the end of the pier.

'No,' he admitted seriously. 'My mistake.' His mouth kinked in a smile that might have been apologetic, but she doubted it. 'Sorry.'

'Sorry?' She didn't want apologies; she wanted more!

Matt hadn't meant to do it. Hadn't meant to kiss her. He'd sworn he wouldn't do anything that would put his mission at risk. Keeping Nyssa safe had to come first. But she hadn't objected. On the contrary. Which was making it doubly difficult to concentrate on the task in hand. 'I was like that as a boy,' he said. 'I always wanted pudding first.'

'And did you get it?'

'You've got to be kidding. My mother was immovable on the subject. Bread and butter before cakes. No exceptions.'

Nyssa thought he was kidding. She hoped he was, but even so she straightened her mouth, put on a disapproving face. 'Your mother was right. And I suggest you stick to mineral water from now on, because you're going to be driving out of here on the stroke of midnight, Cinderella,' she said, attempting

serious affront. Breathlessness, and the certainty that her unrestrained response to his
kiss made the effort redundant, left her words
without any sting in them. 'So forget any idea
of coming back for seconds,' she added, trying harder to sound cross.

'If you insist,' he said, finding it hard to
control the grin that kept trying to break out
all over his face. She didn't mean it. After all,
he was still holding her, still had the scent of
her body filling his head, could still feel the
faintest tremble of her body against his. She
hadn't pulled away, even when she was giving
him his marching orders. 'But it seems a
shame to miss out on all that champagne when
your mother has already offered me a bed for
the night.'

'Oh, no…' Oh, yes!

His smile was wry. 'You're quite safe, I
promise. I may be wrong, but I don't imagine
she was offering me yours…'

'Don't you believe it! There are no depths
she wouldn't sink to—' Nyssa stopped, real-
ising that she was about to betray herself. And

Matt Crosby already knew far too much about her.

'To keep you from casting flirtatious eyes at Gil Paton?' He completed the stalled sentence for her.

Stunned, she could do nothing to hide her shock. 'How do you know about...?' Then, angrily, jerking out of his arms, 'It's not like that!'

'No?'

His voice was so gentle. He was so clever. 'No!' And she turned away from him, presenting him with a stiff back.

'What is it like, Nyssa?' Matt asked, not in the least fazed by her sudden rejection.

'You wouldn't understand.'

'I might. Why don't you try me?'

'You're a psychologist as well as a journalist, are you?'

'I'm someone you can trust.' Parker might not agree, but he wasn't half in love with Parker. 'Whatever else I am, you can believe that.'

She glanced back at him, looking over her shoulder. Then she said, 'Really?' and the uncertainty in her voice, the unspoken yearning, undermined her defiant posture.

She was so strong for her cause, so apparently in control of her life, yet that one word betrayed a personal innocence that left Matt wanting to take her into his arms and hold her, protect her from the physical and emotional demons that haunted her. But before he could do that he needed her total trust.

'Really,' he managed, if a touch hoarsely. Half in love? Who was he kidding?

'Well, you would say that, wouldn't you?' she said, and laughed a little shakily. 'I'd have to be crazy to trust a journalist.'

'There's nothing wrong with being a little crazy once in a while.' He took her hands, turning her to face him as he held them between his, putting everything he felt for her into his grasp. 'Trust me.' He needed her to believe in him. If she believed him, it would make it true.

Nyssa couldn't meet his eyes. Instead she kept her gaze riveted on his hands; they were holding hers tightly, as if he would protect her from the entire world.

Well, he had protected her. He had been there. Gil had come to Delvering not because he loved her, but because his wife had insisted. He'd said so. She just hadn't wanted to hear that. For years she'd been refusing to listen... And Kitty had insisted only to please her father, who would do anything to keep Sophia from worrying about her troublesome daughter.

She should be gratified that she had achieved such success. She was, after all, exactly what she'd set out to be from the moment her mother had remarried: a problem child. Going on twenty-three, it didn't seem to be such a great achievement.

'Come on,' Matt said, as a burst of laughter disturbed the quiet of the garden. 'Let's get out of here. Someone said something about a beach?'

His words seemed to release her. 'You want to paddle?'

'I want to talk. I want to know what you're doing about security. I want to be sure you're safe…'

'Don't be boring, Matt. This is a party. You're supposed to be having a good time.'

'Maybe I should kidnap you myself. That way I'll know you're safe.' He looked around. 'It wouldn't be difficult. I don't suppose anyone would miss you for a while. Your mother would probably think you were with me somewhere. I get the feeling she'd be quite happy with that—'

'Oh, all right! You've made your point.' She pulled away and turned towards the path through the shrubbery. 'It's this way.' And she walked off, leading the way towards the small private beach below the house. But when she stumbled in her high heels he caught her, steadied her, and she made no objection to his hand at her waist, even though she kicked off her shoes and walked barefoot down the steep wooden steps.

At that point Matt knew that, consciously or not, she had made the decision to trust him. It didn't make him feel anywhere near as good as it should have done.

CHAPTER SIX

'WELL?' Nyssa demanded irritably, flinging herself down onto the soft sand. Matt sank down beside her, leaning back against his elbows, looking out at a sea silvered by the rising moon. Behind them the low cliff guarded their backs and the feeling of total isolation was broken only by an occasional burst of music carried on the breeze. Siren sounds that temptingly hinted that this was a time, a place, for love.

'You've known Gil Paton for a long time, I imagine,' he said, casually enough, but he felt an increase in the tension emanating from her like a force field. He wanted to hold her, reassure her... Of what? That everything would be all right? How could he tell her that? He had no confidence in 'all right' happening. 'He served with your father? In the army?'

Nyssa had hoped he'd leave it. Despite giving him his marching orders, she longed for him to take her in his arms and finish what they'd begun in Delvering. Crazy, maybe. But it was a warm night, with a full, lover's moon over the sea. And they had the beach to themselves.

It could be a lot crazier.

But instead Matt persisted in talking about Gil and her father, for heaven's sake!

And she'd doubted that he was a journalist?

'Why do you want to know? Does this come under the heading of ''Background Material''? It sounds a little personal to me.' She definitely didn't want to talk about Gil. 'Tell me, Matt, what kind of article are you hoping to write?'

'It comes under whatever heading you like, but it won't be going into any magazine. You can count on it.'

'Can I?' she challenged him. 'Can I count on *you*?'

He turned to glance at her and, despite the defiant way she held her head, the raw, aggressive tone in her voice, her eyes betrayed her. Her eyes held the kind of desperate need that would send a man who valued his independence running for cover. It was a look that told him she needed someone who would be there for her. Someone who would always put her first.

'Whatever you hear, whatever anyone tells you, believe this...' He held her gaze and listened to himself pledge his life away. 'I will be there for you for as long as you need me.' There was an endless moment in which the only sound was that of the waves lapping at the shore a few yards away from them. She was very still, as if she was absorbing the weight of his words, their meaning. Then, as if the tension was suddenly too much, she lifted her hand as if to brush away something she couldn't see.

'Don't...'

'Don't what?'

'Don't pretend.'

He sat up, propping his arms on his knees as he turned to her. 'No pretence. Just a promise. I won't leave your side until this thing at Delvering is over.' It was true. He'd protect her from physical danger in any way he could. His methods might not win her undying gratitude. He had the feeling that at the end of this, he wasn't going to be in anyone's good books. He just hoped that when she realised, understood what he'd done, she'd know that counting on him would always be the right choice.

'You think they'll try again?' she asked.

'I think—' he began, then shrugged. 'I think you shouldn't take any chances.' He picked up a shell, tossed it towards the sea. And offered her an escape route. 'Perhaps you'd be happier asking your brother-in-law for help?'

'No,' she said quickly. 'No. Gil has other things on his mind. Kitty—his wife—is expecting another baby.' Matt said nothing, and she wrapped her arms about her knees and rested her chin on them, staring out to sea. 'He loves her so much.'

'It must be hard for you.'

'What can't be cured must be endured.'
Then, startled, she turned her head to look at
him.

'I'm a good listener.'

'It goes with the job, I imagine,' she said
slowly.

'Forget the job. I'm not taking notes.'

'You mean this is off the record?' He said
nothing, just crossed his heart with his finger
and Nyssa sighed. 'The first time I saw Gil I
was seven years old. Dad invited him home
for the weekend and he brought me a cuddly
toy. A soft white rabbit with pink paws and
floppy ears.'

'Do you still keep it on your bed?'

'Who said I ever did?' She lay back on the
sand, careless of her dress, her hair, staring up
at the night sky. 'You're right,' she said, when
he didn't answer. 'Of course I put it on my
bed. It stayed there until Gil's first child,
Harry, was born. Then I put it away. Wrapped
it in tissue and put it at the back of the cupboard along with all my childish things.'
Along with her heart.

'Burying things, feelings, can make them take on an importance out of all proportion, Nyssa.'

She glanced at him. 'You want me to talk about it, Mr Psychologist? Is that it? Pour out my heart and soul?'

'It might help.'

Nyssa stared up at the stars and wondered about that. The way she'd felt about Gil had always been locked inside her head. Even now, she was sure that saying the words out loud would reduce what had always seemed very special to nothing but a childish crush. Something rather silly. But she told him anyway.

How she'd followed Gil around that first day, like some adoring puppy, until her father had taken him down to the pub so that he could have some peace. How she'd told her mother she was going to marry him when she grew up.

Her mother had laughed and told her father, and he had laughed too.

'Kids say that kind of stuff,' Matt said.

'Kids grow out of it.' But she hadn't. She'd even refused to be bridesmaid when he had married his first wife, Elizabeth, crying herself to sleep for weeks, even before she knew exactly what she was crying for. 'After Gil married, we didn't see him much. Then Dad...' She took a breath. 'Then Dad was killed and he came straight away.'

'How old were you?'

'Thirteen.' She glared at him, daring to make the obvious point about losing her father at a difficult age and Gil being there. She knew all the psychobabble.

Matt simply said, 'That must have been hard for you.' He didn't specify which pain had been the more difficult to bear.

'Yes,' she said huskily, swallowing back tears that had suddenly welled up from nowhere, taking her by surprise. She didn't cry. She didn't! 'And then, a year later, Gil's wife left him.'

Out of the darkness, Matt's hand grasped hers. 'Too young,' he said, understanding without her having to explain.

'But not too young to know what I wanted. Not too young to hope that he might stick around long enough for me to grow up. Except that when I was eighteen he met my new stepfather's daughter, Kitty Lambert. An actress, for heaven's sake!' she exploded. Glamorous, beautiful, and he'd fallen for her like a ton of bricks. Not that she'd blamed him for that—who wouldn't fall for Kitty? And once more Nyssa had cried her pillow into a soggy lump and consoled herself with the certainty that it wouldn't last. 'It shouldn't have lasted.' Actresses were fickle, changeable creatures, weren't they? She'd given it three months, tops. 'But it did.'

After three months there had been the wedding, then Harry, sweet adorable Harry, had been born. And Kitty wasn't like Elizabeth. No matter how hard she tried, Nyssa couldn't hate her; she knew Kitty loved Gil, would die for him as he would die for her.

Matt didn't condemn her. Nor did he laugh. And he was right about being a good listener. He heard a lot more than she was telling him.

'There's been no one for you? No one at all?' he asked, after a pause that seemed to stretch for ever. 'Not even as a grandstanding gesture with some utterly unsuitable man in an attempt to get him to notice you? To say... You could have had this?'

She turned then, to look at him, confront the slight frown that puckered his brow. 'I was wrong about you, Matt,' she said, shivering a little as she sat up. He took off his jacket and put it around her shoulders, leaving his arm about her so that it was the most natural thing in the world to lean against him. 'You understand all too well.'

'No one?' he persisted, refusing to be distracted.

To answer him truthfully would be to expose herself entirely. But then, she'd told him everything else. All the secrets of her heart. And in the quiet dark of the beach it seemed that there was nothing she couldn't tell him, no secret she wouldn't trust him with. 'No one. The other night at Delvering was the closest I've ever...' The longing grabbed at her and she turned to look up at him, willing him to kiss her, take her. Now, she thought. Do it now!

But he didn't move. Didn't even look at her. 'That was a natural reaction to danger, Nyssa. It meant nothing.'

Nothing? Nothing to him, maybe. 'No,' she said carelessly. 'Of course it didn't.' She tossed off the jacket, turned and knelt in front of him, forcing him to look at her. 'But I'm not in any danger now, Matt.' Damn her voice for trembling, giving her away. She would do this, lay this ghost that Matt had dredged up, and he would help her. She reached out, touched his cheek with her fingertips, trailed them provocatively across his mouth.

Matt was ready to explode. Nothing! He'd heard himself say that and still didn't know how he'd made himself say the word. If she'd known more, known to touch him... She wanted him to make the decision, wanted him to take the responsibility and push her, take her all the way, and it would be so easy.

He'd been strong once, resisted temptation, the desire that swarmed through his blood like a virus. Twice was too much to expect...

He stopped the traitorous, tempting thought. He'd resist twice, three times, as many times as it took for her to come to him, to want him for himself, not as some second-best lover whose only purpose would be to overwrite a desire that could never be fulfilled. Sweating with the effort, he forced himself to contemplate the horrors of making love on sand.

He could put down his jacket...

'Are you sure?' he asked roughly, while he could still speak, still think. He wanted her, more than anything in the world he wanted her, but not like this. He grabbed at her wrist to stop the insidious persuasion of her fingers against his skin. 'Do you really want *me*, Nyssa? Do you really trust me? Or is it just that your hormones have finally had a taste of the action and are demanding some serious attention?'

For a moment she stared at him, scarcely able to believe that he'd rejected her again.

Then she leapt to her feet, showering him with sand. 'Damn you, Matt Crosby!'

He should be relieved. He wasn't. He felt hollow, but he kept pushing her. 'I thought so. It was just an experiment for you, and any man would do for that.'

'If any man would have done…' She caught the words. 'I thought you were different. I thought you actually cared.'

He cared, far too much to do what she wanted. But she didn't wait for him to explain. Instead she swung around and ran down to the edge of the sea where the water washed in white ripples about her ankles.

Cold water. Good choice. If she'd stormed back up to the house he'd have stripped off and flung himself into the sea. The only alternative was putting some distance between them.

He would have preferred distance, distance would have been easier, but he'd appointed himself her protector and he couldn't leave her alone on the beach. It seemed deserted, but the low cliff was full of shadows and the illusion of safety was just that. An illusion. The house was full of people, not just guests, but musicians, caterers—who would notice a few more men in white jackets? Back in the garden he'd joked about how easy it would be to spirit her away. It wasn't, he discovered, that funny.

He got to his feet, shook off the sand—he'd been right about that at least, he thought. The beach was no place to erase girlish dreams of sexual bliss with the object of her infatuation. It would require careful planning, the perfect atmosphere; it would have to be a champagne and roses affair, a night at the Ritz... The Paris Ritz.

Which ruled him out—he couldn't afford it!

He would have to console himself with the certainty that a quick deflowering was not the answer for Nyssa. She would hate herself afterwards. And him.

She'd probably hate him anyway when she found out who he was. At least this way she'd know he hadn't taken advantage of her in a weak moment. Maybe, a long time in the future, when she'd calmed down, she would re-member that and think of him kindly for it.

He pulled off his shoes and socks and headed for the surf. 'Damn it, it's cold,' he said, as the water swirled around his ankles.

She shrugged. 'Isn't that the answer to an overheated libido? Cold water?'

'Only a temporary one. Unless you fancy hypothermia?'

'Isn't there some kind of compromise?' When he didn't answer, she offered him a slightly rueful smile. 'I'm sorry, Matt. You're right, of course. I just wanted you to take the responsibility.'

'That's honest. Cruel,' he added, with a wry grin of his own, 'but honest. Actually, I don't have a problem with honesty. Honesty I can take to bed with a clear conscience,' he sug-gested, mock hopefully, practically gagging on the words.

She finally relaxed, shook her head. 'No. You're right. Forget it.' And she turned her face to the sea. 'Much more sensible to leave it at supper and a night on the sofa-bed—' she glanced up at him '—if you still want to stay? Maybe in the morning—'

'In the morning?' he leapt in, continuing to make a joke of it.

She didn't laugh. 'In the morning,' she continued seriously, 'we can discuss this in-depth article you want to write. You wanted to join the Save the Gaumont group, learn about the way we work first-hand? Isn't that what you said? Are you still interested?'

'I'm still interested,' he said evenly. A lot more than interested. Matt looked down into her disturbing blue eyes and called himself every kind of a fool. 'And if I tag along I'll be able to keep an eye out for those thugs who jumped you.'

The moonlight washed out the subtle contours of her face, but he thought she looked relieved. 'I was hoping you'd say that.'

'It'll make a good story.'

'Yes,' she said, with a slight catch at her breath. 'Of course it will.' Then, polite, cool, oddly formal, 'You'd know them again?'

'Yes, I'd know them.'

She nodded. 'It's a deal, then.'

'It's a deal.' And he held out his hand. After a moment's hesitation she took it, held it lightly. Her fingers were cool but her touch ran like a torch up his arm… 'Can we go back to the party now?' he said quickly, releasing her. 'My feet are freezing.'

'Anything a dance would fix?'

Very probably. It was conceivable that dancing with Nyssa Blake would reduce even Jack Frost to a warm puddle. 'Actually, I was thinking of something more along the lines of a large Scotch,' he said.

For some reason that made Nyssa smile. 'No problem,' she said, turning to hook her arm through his. 'A large Scotch and something to eat. Then we'll have that dance. You haven't forgotten you asked me for a dance?'

'In a moment of weakness.'

'It won't be that bad.'

It would be that bad. It would be torture. Sweet torture, but torture nonetheless. He wondered if she realised that and was paying him back a little for his earlier rejection of her.

If so, the next week or two were going to be difficult. Interesting, but difficult.

Matt woke to the sound of a cup being placed on the table beside him, and he opened his eyes just sufficiently to let in the light.

Nyssa was bent over, looking at him in a way that suggested she'd said something and expected a response. For the moment, though, he was content to enjoy the sight of her long tanned legs, revealed in all their glory by the thigh-skimming T-shirt she'd worn to bed.

Her hair was still rumpled, her eyes sleepily sexy, and, thinking him still asleep, she reached out and gently stroked the edge of his ear with the tip of one finger. In another time, another life, he'd have responded to his instincts and tumbled her down beside him on the sofa.

'Matt?'

Her voice, uncertain, just a bit nervous, put his libido on hold, and he groaned as if only just stirring. 'What?' And he opened his eyes.

'I said, wake up, sleepyhead. Fine watch dog you are.'

He didn't move. 'You said one dance. I'm not used to this kind of fast living.'

Nyssa laughed, relaxed. 'Yesterday was nothing. Today it's Harry's turn, so you'd better get this coffee down you while I take a shower.' As she said the word she plainly remembered making him a promise about a shower, and she backed away, blushing with confusion. 'I...um...won't be long.'

He lifted his head so as not to miss a single moment of her retreat into the bedroom. 'Do we have to stay?'

She had legs to die for and the neatest backside that would fit so perfectly into his palms as he pulled her close... His body remembered how she'd melted against his in time to the music, her arms entwined about his neck. She'd needed someone to hold her, help her forget that Gil Paton was dancing with his pregnant wife a few feet away. He'd been handy, that was all. To imagine more was to invite heartbreak. But it had taken hours for his body to climb down, forgive him. Sleep had been hard won, and his head ached with the hours of tension.

'Couldn't we creep out the back way while everyone's still thinking about breakfast?'

'Wimp,' she said, but not unkindly, as she stopped and turned to face him, clinging to the doorframe, half hiding behind it. 'James and Gil will already be down on the beach, building the barbecue. And they're both older than you.'

'Oh, well, never let it be said that I can't pull my weight in the sandcastle-building department. You've got two minutes in that shower.'

She didn't move, just smiled. 'Thanks.'

'What for?'

'Last night. Everything.' Then she was gone and a moment later he heard the water running. He forced himself to reach out for the coffee, and drink it very slowly.

'Matt.' He turned as Gil Paton joined him at the barbecue.

'Gil,' he responded laconically, concentrating on turning over the spiced chicken wings he'd been charged with keeping an eye on.

'I was hoping to catch you on your own.'

'You've got me. What's your problem?'

'Nyssa.' He said it as if it had been the burden of a lifetime. 'What really happened at Delvering?'

'Happened? A few thugs broke up the meeting. Nothing to get into a sweat over.'

'I wanted to stay, but she's so damned stubborn.' Gil shrugged. 'I thought she seemed a bit jittery last night, though. It isn't like her and I wondered if there was more to it.'

Matt thought that Gil Paton could have put a stop to Nyssa's hero-worship a long time ago by behaving a little less heroically, caring a little less obviously, by being prepared to sacrifice her good opinion of him.

'You needn't worry about Nyssa, Gil. She's not a child any more.'

Paton stiffened imperceptibly. 'I know that. But I've known her a long time—'

'Since she was a little girl and you bought her a toy rabbit. I know; she told me.' He looked up then. 'She's all grown up now. And she's got me to look after her.'

From the far side of the beach Nyssa watched Matt and Gil as they stood by the barbecue. They were pretty much of a height, but Matt was leaner, darker. They looked so serious. Gil was undoubtedly grilling him about the meeting at Delvering and she wondered, anxiously, what Matt would say; she should have warned him not to tell anyone what had really happened.

Matt saw her looking, caught the question in her eyes and with the smallest shake of his head reassured her.

'Where did you find him?' Kitty asked, grinning as she followed her gaze.

'I didn't. He found me.'

'Lucky you. He's absolutely gorgeous. I can see why you can't take your eyes off him.'

'Gorgeous, but dangerous,' her mother warned, watching the two men through narrowed eyes. 'You'll never know what he's thinking until it's too late to do anything about it.'

Nyssa had the uneasy feeling that Sophia was right, but, aware that Matt was watching her, she made a drinking motion with her hand behind the women's backs. 'You're dead wrong. I can read his mind. Any minute now he's going to come over here and ask if we want a drink.' Right on cue, Matt handed the cooking fork to Gil and, extracting some cans of soda from the coldbox, headed in their direction.

'You look hot, ladies.' He handed around the drinks and ripped the tab from his own can, lifting an eyebrow in gentle query as he passed one to her. 'Why don't you take a rest while we make some sandcastles? What d'you say, Harry?'

'I don't know about Harry, but I think you're a hero,' Kitty said.

'Not me. There's too much competition around here. I just like making sandcastles. Nyssa? You want to give me a hand? You've had a lot more experience of entrenchment than me.'

'Very funny,' she said, but nevertheless picked up a small spade and began to fill a bucket. Kitty and her mother drifted away to settle in deckchairs. 'Sophia thinks you're dangerous,' Nyssa said, after a while.

'Oh? Did she say why?'

'Only that I'd never know what you're thinking until it was too late.'

'Too late for what?' he demanded.

Nyssa pushed back her bright fringe with her arm, leaving a smear of damp sand across her forehead. 'I don't know, but with that build-up, I'm relying on you not to disappoint me.'

'I'll try not to. But I'm leaving for London right after we've eaten. Are you coming with me or staying here?'

'There are other alternatives.'

'No, Nyssa, there aren't. Not if you were serious about wanting me to watch your back. Not until we find out who was behind the incident at Delvering.'

'I have to be in Delvering tomorrow for a planning meeting. I'll follow you...'

'I'd rather you came with me. Too many people know your car.'

He'd expected an argument, but she just nodded. 'I'm going to stay there overnight. I need to get inside the cinema somehow.' She waited for him to ask what 'somehow' meant. He didn't bother. 'Does that fit in with your plans?'

'From now on your plans are my plans. Besides, I'd like to see what all the fuss is about.'

'It's boarded up,' she warned him. 'There's a security guard.'

'Are you telling me that's a problem?'

'Er, no,' she said. Then grinned. 'Oh, here come the rest of the family, now everything is finished. Lazy lot.' But she was laughing as she said it.

'You've missed one.'

'Thanks, Matt.' Nyssa's mother looked up from the shoreline and took the shell he handed her and dropped it in the little plastic bucket she was carrying. He fell in beside her. 'Harry wants shells to decorate the sandcastles but there don't seem to be many. Have you had a good day?'

'A good weekend, thanks. We'll be leaving soon, though.'

Sophia stopped, looked at him. 'You'll look after her, won't you, Matt?'

'With my last breath,' he promised. 'But in the meantime there's something you can do for her.' And as they walked slowly along the edge of the sea, the water lapping around their feet, Matt told Sophia exactly who he was, what he was doing in Delvering. What had happened.

'I don't understand. Why didn't Nyssa tell me about the kidnapping? Gil…'

'She doesn't want Gil involved. She doesn't want you to worry.'

Sophia smiled. 'Are you sure? That doesn't sound much like my daughter.'

'She doesn't want you to worry you about this because it's serious. I have no choice.'

And then he told her about the information he'd uncovered. And what Parker would do with it when he found out.

'But Nyssa doesn't know her father invested in those shares in that construction company.'

'That won't matter to the press, Sophia, and there isn't much time. Parker is going to get impatient very quickly. And then he'll get someone else to do his dirty work for him. You're the one in control of the money—'

'Is there anything you *didn't* find out?' He stopped and Sophia took his hand. 'I'm sorry, go on.'

'I hoped you'd be in a position to have the shares sold. And quickly.'

'I'll see to it first thing.' She carried on walking. 'I'm glad you told me. I knew who you were, of course. Someone at the party recognised you, had a word with James.'

There had been at least a dozen people at the party he'd recognised, had once been on at least nodding acquaintance with. None of them had felt inclined to acknowledge the fact.

'So why wasn't I thrown out on my ear?'

'Because you're Nyssa's friend and she's entitled to make her own mistakes.' Then she stopped and turned to face him. 'Not that I believe you're a mistake. As James said, you can tell an awful lot about a man from the enemies he makes.'

CHAPTER SEVEN

'YOU were getting very pally, shell-collecting with my mother,' Nyssa said as he drove towards London. 'What were you talking about?'

'She worries about you.' He glanced at her and, hoping to divert her, he said, 'I imagine that's the intention?'

'That's a rotten thing to say.' But evidently near enough the truth for her to turn away, open the glove compartment and fish out the open packet of biscuits. 'Rotten, but true.'

She offered him one, but he shook his head. 'They're supposed to be for emergencies.'

'This *is* an emergency. I'm baring my soul here, and for that I need chocolate.' She bit into one. 'Ugh, these are soft.'

'If it was an emergency you wouldn't care.'

She pulled a face and ate it, like a little girl scolded for wasting food, but he wasn't fooled

for a moment. She was playing for time, trying to decide what to tell him and what she
could leave out. Deciding what bits of her soul
she preferred to keep from him. He didn't
hurry her, keeping his gaze fixed firmly on he
road.

'When my mother married James I was angry, really angry.' He didn't need to ask why;
he could guess. 'I idolised my father. He was
a hero. He was decorated.' She turned to see
what effect this revelation had upon him.
'Posthumously,' she declared.

'I know.'

'Of course you do. You're a journalist and
you've done all the background research.' Not
him, but someone had. And they'd been very
thorough. 'I went to the palace with my
mother to get his medal.'

'I saw the picture,' he murmured, recalling
the pale-faced teenager staring into the camera
as her mother paused politely for a photogra-
pher. She didn't appear to hear him.

'I mean, how dared she marry someone
else?'

'Maybe she was lonely?' Matt suggested. Nyssa blinked, concentrated on licking the chocolate off her fingers. 'There should be some tissues...'

She found them, wiped her fingers, lifted her shoulders in an awkward little shrug. 'I suppose she was. What do children know about how adults hurt? They're big and strong and shouldn't ever need anyone.'

'Nyssa—'

'It gave me the biggest buzz ever to get arrested for causing a breach of the peace at a demonstration while they were on honeymoon. The most inordinate pleasure that they had to interrupt their idyll to bail me out.'

'They should have left you to stew.'

She glanced across at him. 'Is that what you'd have done? '

'Let's hope we never have to find out.'

'No. Well. That was years ago—it's not like that now. Not any more.'

He thought perhaps it was just a little bit like that still, but he didn't want her angry at him so he said, 'Well, I can see that you're all grown up now. Family lunches, cricket on the beach, very civilised, very sweet.' She said something very rude, but not with any serious intent, and he laughed, as he suspected he was meant to. 'Perhaps not that grown up.'

'I'm working on it. Really.' And she gave him a look that fanned the embers of a fire he was doing his level best to keep damped down. It would be so easy to let nature take its course. Do what she wanted. Too easy. He'd never been able to settle for second best. He wanted her heart as well as her body. Given freely, with love.

When he held her in his arms and made a woman of her he wanted her to be thinking only of him. No ghosts. No regrets. Total commitment.

Nothing less would do.

Matt stooped to pick up the package lying on his doormat and pushed it into his pocket. It would keep. He preferred to watch Nyssa as she walked around the living room of his small rented flat, her fingertips brushing over the furniture as if reading the ambience of the place from the worn fibres of the sofa, the scarred surface of a table.

Her hair slid from her neck as she bent to turn on a lamp. Immediately the place seemed brighter, warmer. Or maybe that was just the glow imparted by her very presence. She was like a perfect piece of porcelain. Delicate, fragile, lovely, so vulnerable that he was afraid she might break.

It was an illusion, he knew, and yet he ached to reach out to her, protect her, cradle her in his arms and blot out the hideous flat. Blot out the world.

Or maybe he was fooling himself. Maybe he was the one in need of comfort, his ache simply self-pity for all that he had lost, like his huge loft apartment overlooking the river, with its acres of polished wood floor, fine rugs, pictures. It would have made a proper setting for such an extraordinary woman.

For the first time in as long as he could remember he found himself wanting to tell someone what had happened to his life. To say... What you're seeing here, this isn't me. I'm someone else entirely. But he held his tongue. He'd done what he had to do and paid for it, was still paying, but it had been his choice. No excuses.

She turned, lifted her hand to her hair, sliding her fingers through it as she pushed it back from her face. He knew the silky feel of it against his hand, his face. He knew the scent of her skin, the taste of her mouth, warm and salty from the damp sea air. He knew how her arms felt about his neck and the press of her body against his in the crush of the dance floor. He would never forget any of it.

She continued her exploration, opening the bedroom door, smiling back at him in a way that lit the place up. Lit him up.

'Only one bed?' she asked.

The ache deepened, intensified, altered, so it was something else entirely. 'That's usually enough,' he managed, through a throat thick with desire. 'I'll take the sofa. Again.'

'I'll toss you for it?' she offered, neatly dealing with any lingering regrets he might be having about turning her down. In the Delvering Arms. And on the beach. When they'd finally left the party to those who had nothing better to do than stay up all night, she'd pointed him in the direction of the sofa in her small top-floor flat, and closed the bedroom door without lingering to see if he'd had a change of heart. Well, no girl was going to offer a man more than two chances. Not unless he was on his knees, begging.

'You'll be sorry if you lose,' he said.

'No, I won't. You're a gentleman; you'd insist I have the bed anyway.'

'Not that much of a gentleman.' His shrug was a calculated masterpiece of understatement. 'I'd offer to share, though.'

'Have a care, Crosby. I might not refuse and then what would you do?' she teased.

Suffer. But there was absolutely no way she was going to lose, he promised himself as he extracted a coin from his pocket. He tossed it in the air and clamped it against the back of his hand.

'Your call,' he said.

'Heads.'

He raised his hand slightly to check the coin. 'It must be your lucky day.'

'Show me.'

'What is this?' he demanded. 'You don't trust me?' He kept his hand over the coin and glanced up at her. 'You're only supposed to complain if you lose.'

'Injured innocence doesn't suit you, Matt,' she said.

'No? It's only got one head, I promise you.' He tossed the coin again, caught it and flipped it to her. 'See for yourself.' Whether it had landed face up was for him to know and her to live with, whether she believed him or not. And if she offered to share with him he'd say no. Right? 'The bathroom's through there. Coffee?' he offered, turning away, needing to put some space between the bed, himself and her before the tempting juxtaposition gave him some seriously reckless ideas.

'I'd rather have tea.' She followed him into the cramped kitchen, watched as he opened a battered tea caddy. There were half a dozen leaves in the bottom. 'Is that a problem?'

The problem was that she was standing way too close, her arm pressed against his as she leaned over to peer in the empty caddy. 'I don't get many visitors, but, no, it's not a problem. There's a place on the corner that never seems to close,' he said, retreating from the intimacy, pulling on his jacket. 'I won't be long. Is there anything else I should get? For breakfast?' he added quickly, before she thought he was suggesting something else entirely.

'Bread.' She opened his fridge, took out a carton of milk and sniffed at it gingerly. She pulled a face and put it on the draining board. 'Milk, butter, eggs. What were you planning for supper?' she asked, turning to him.

'Pizza? It has all the major food groups,' he said, when she looked doubtful. 'And the advantage of requiring no more effort than a phone call.'

'That's no fun.'

'It makes me happy.'

'Oh, come on…' She glanced around. 'I mean, we've got to do something to fill the time, and since you don't appear to have a television—' he'd never felt the need before '—how are we going to entertain ourselves?'

'You could tell me how you got involved in the campaign to save the Gaumont.'

She pulled a face. 'As if you're interested.' Then, 'You could tell me your life story?' she countered hopefully.

'I just remembered that I love to cook.'

She gave him a disbelieving look. 'And here was me thinking that the yearning to bake came ready packaged only with the female chromosomes. You learn something new every day.' She gave his cupboards a cursory glance, found some pasta that was past its sell-by date and dropped it in the bin, making her point before dusting off her hands. 'Of course you could be lying. I think I'd better come shopping with you.'

'I'd prefer you to stay here. You might be recognised.' Might was understating the situation. Nyssa Blake was a woman once seen, never forgotten.

'You're not suggesting my would-be kidnappers will be staking out your corner shop on the off-chance I'll stop by for a packet of tea?' She didn't come right out and say she thought he was crazy, but the inflection of the voice, her expression, implied it. 'How would they know who you are?'

If they'd been Parker's men, and they still could be, they'd know.

Okay, it was unlikely they'd be waiting at the corner of the street. But then the whole thing seemed unlikely. If he'd hadn't been at Delvering, been in the thick of it, he'd have been very sceptical about the whole incident. Maybe he was a cynic, but he'd have assumed it was all just an elaborate publicity stunt, stacking the odds on front-page coverage for what, in the global scheme of things, was a very minor cause.

That was still a possibility, Matt reminded himself. Cynically. Then, recalling the way Nyssa had lashed out at him while she believed him to be one of the kidnappers, the way she had dissolved in his arms as reality had hit home, he pushed the thought away. He didn't want that to have been an act.

If it had been, why would she be with him, in his flat?

'Trust me,' he said. 'If you make a personal appearance it'll be around the neighbourhood in half an hour flat. Then the press will find out where you are. And then everyone will know.'

'I can't imagine ''everyone'' will be that interested.'

'Not everyone. But someone will be.'

She tried to outstare him, but failed. 'You're forgetting that I'm a master of disguise,' she said, as her gaze faltered.

'Just make a list, Nyssa. And if you want to do something useful—' This was a memo to himself, as much as to her. It was time to put all thought of her naked in his arms on hold and get on with the job of keeping her safe. 'If you want to do something really useful, get in touch with Sky—you've got your laptop with you. She made a note of everyone arriving at the Assembly Rooms the other night and I'd like a look at that list.'

She shrugged. 'Okay, I'll have her e-mail it to me. Or maybe she could bring it over and we could all—'

'No. I'd prefer to keep this address just between the two of us.' She lifted her brows at his sharp tone. 'It's comforting to have a bolthole. Somewhere no one knows about.' Before she could object, he dug around in his jacket pocket and produced two cellphones. One his own, the other the one he'd bought with the spare change from Parker's money. That was the one he gave her. 'Use this. It's new and the number can't be traced back to either of us.'

'And I thought I was paranoid.'

She didn't take the phone, and he placed it on the small table that he used as a desk. 'You put yourself in my care, Nyssa. If you're having second thoughts, say so now and I'll call you a taxi.'

'A taxi? I don't even get a lift? What happened to Sir Galahad?'

'If you don't trust me, you shouldn't put yourself at that kind of risk.' She didn't respond. 'It's okay, Nyssa. I understand. It's a tough call.' He opened the drawer of a small work-table tucked in an alcove and took out his spare door key. 'Maybe you'll feel safer with this.' He took her hand, placed the key in her palm and wrapped her fingers about it.

She opened her hand, looked at the key and frowned. 'This is the key to your flat?'

'It's not much, but it's safe. For now.'

'Matt, are you warning me not to trust Sky?'

'I'm simply advising you to take the simplest precautions. All I know about Sky is that she's got a nice smile. It's not much of a character reference.' He could see that she didn't like what he was saying. He'd scarcely begun. 'You'd better put that in your pocket,' he said, and when she didn't he took it from her and tucked it into the change pocket at the waist of her jeans. The wear-softened cloth was warm from her skin, and his fingers were tempted to linger, but Nyssa pulled away.

'This is silly. I don't need to hide from Sky.'

'Probably not.' Then, 'How long have you known her? Where did you meet? Did she approach you?'

'What—?'

'Just how far would you trust her? Or any of your group?' As he piled up the questions, making a point, putting the doubts in her mind, he could see that, far from planting doubts about Sky, he was the one she was suddenly wary of. Well, that was no bad thing. She should be wary of everyone right now. Close enough to feel the nervous catch of her breath against his neck, he reached up and stroked his thumb against her cheek, a gesture at once gentle and threatening. 'With your life?' he asked, pressing home the message.

She flinched, shivered, but stood her ground, lifting her chin with a touch of bravado. 'You're being over-dramatic,' she declared. 'This isn't about life and death. It's about money.'

'There's a difference?'

She shook her head. 'I trust Sky. Absolutely. I know her. You're the only mystery in my life.'

He offered a wry smile. 'You're learning fast.'

'Am I? I'm here, alone with you.'

'And are you afraid?'

She didn't hesitate. 'Oh, yes, Matt.' And it was her turn to raise her hand to his face, rub her palm against his jaw. 'I'm afraid that you're going to hurt me a lot more than Parker's bullies ever could.'

'Not if I can help it.'

Her mouth hinted at a smile, no more. 'Is that why you lied about the coin toss? You did lie, didn't you?' she persisted. His silence was all the answer she needed. 'We could share that bed, Matt. We shared in Delvering.'

'We didn't have a sofa in—'

'Shhh,' she said, stopping the words with her fingers to his lips. Then she put her hands on his shoulders, raised herself onto her toes, leaned into him and touched her mouth to his.

The kiss began innocently enough. It was a real old-fashioned, girl-next-door kiss; nothing at all for the censors to get into a lather about. And for a moment he thought that was it. Maybe that was all she meant it to be.

But her lips parted softly on a sigh and she breathed her sweetness into his mouth, her slender body swaying against his, light as thistledown. He felt a tremor sweep through her and the sigh became more, much more.

His arms, with a will of their own, encircled her waist, holding her, keeping her close. Keeping her safe, he promised himself, even as his hands spread across her back, his thumbs brushed against the swelling of her breasts beneath the thin cotton of her shirt.

From one of them there escaped a soft, urgent sound, and then the tip of her tongue touched lightly against his teeth, a hammer-blow at the door to his soul. Their tongues briefly tangled, bittersweet torture as he fought to hold back from the swirling, tearing need she could provoke with a look. She was tempting him, urging him to accept all that she was offering, sweep her away on the roller coaster she seemed hell-bent on riding to oblivion. Begging him to forget his good intentions and count the world well lost for a night with Nyssa Blake.

At that moment Matt knew she was wrong. Dead wrong.

That they would be lovers seemed as inevitable as breathing. Only not now. Not here in this miserable little flat. Not if he could help it. But soon—and for a while she would be his. She'd lie in his arms and he'd give her everything he had. Heart, body, soul and finally her freedom. Because once she looked up, having broken free of the past, and saw all the possibilities that life offered a woman like her, she'd soar away into a new, golden future.

And he was the one who would be left on the ground, hurting.

From somewhere he found the strength to break off a kiss that he never wanted to stop.

For a long moment she clung to him, as if she didn't want to ever let go. Then, her fingers slipping from his neck to lie against his chest, she leaned back, looked up into his face.

'Who are you, Matt Crosby?' she asked, her voice cobwebby with unfulfilled desire.

'I'm nobody,' he said harshly. 'Just a hack journalist doing a story on the great Nyssa Blake.' Trust me, he'd said. And had lied without hesitation. But for her sake he had to stick to the plot. 'A hack journalist who's going to collapse from hunger if you don't write that shopping list.'

One who might go crazy if he didn't soon get a blast of cold, fresh air to clear his head. But there was no hope of that. He'd have to make do with warm, Sunday-night-in-the-city air, stale with traffic fumes. Anything, just as long as he put some distance between them.

'I haven't got anything to write with,' she said.

He finally released her and, taking a ball-point pen out of his jacket pocket, he clicked it and handed it to her. His hand appeared steady enough, he noted. Maybe it was the rest of the world that was shaking.

Nyssa lifted one corner of her lovely mouth, tucking it into a smile as she took the pen from him. 'Or anything to write on.' He found the hand-out he'd been given by Sky in his pocket and gave her that. 'It must be tough, being a good guy,' she said, as she began to jot down the list.

He didn't feel good, far from it, but since she clearly didn't expect an answer he wasn't obliged to own up.

'Oh, and for your information, I met Sky on that first demo—'

'The one where you were arrested?'

She looked up, clearly irritated that he'd remembered. 'Do you like risotto?'

'Sure.'

She added a couple of items to the list. 'She took me under her wing, took care of me, showed me the ropes.' She looked up. 'Sky's one hundred per cent committed to saving the world from the vandals, Matt. It's her life.'

'And what about you, Nyssa?'

'Me? What about me?'

'Well, if you carry on like this, in twenty years from now you'll be just like her. How do you feel about that?'

Startled, she held his gaze for a moment. Then she handed him the list.

It wasn't true, of course. Nyssa Blake was nothing like her lieutenant. She had joined in with the nearest protest not out of passion for a cause, but as a cry of pain at the hand life had dealt her. The loss of her father. A youthful infatuation that should have been long outgrown but which fate had conspired to hold her in thrall to.

As he crossed the road, heading for the corner shop, Matt reached in his pocket for his own cellphone and checked his messages. They were all from Charles Parker. So much for being one of the good guys, Matt thought as he called back.

The only claim he'd have to that title rested upon his ability to rescue her from the mess she was in. And perhaps, in the process, help her break the ties that were holding her back, stopping her from becoming a complete woman.

If he had to live with the backwash of pain, well, so be it. Sacrifice was what made the difference between lust and love.

Nyssa was perched on a stool at the tiny breakfast counter, staring at the screen of her laptop, when she heard a key in the door. Despite her earlier bravado, Sky's e-mail had shaken her. Matt had seemed like her white knight. Suddenly she wasn't so sure, and a quick look around the flat did nothing to reassure her. It was anonymous, almost, she thought, unlived-in. Except for a wardrobe full of expensive clothes, a stack of books and a locked steel filing cabinet hidden away in a cupboard and bolted to the floor.

Matt appeared in the kitchen door, his arm around a grocery sack, a smile on his face. 'Sorry I was so long. I've got everything. Even your Earl Grey teabags.'

'Terrific.' She deleted Sky's note with a touch to the keypad, and hoped he didn't pick up the slight wobble in her voice. She had no reason to fear him, she reminded herself. He had rescued her from heaven alone knew what…but he was lying to her about being a journalist. 'The kettle's boiled,' she said, not moving from her perch.

'Is that a hint that I'm supposed to make the tea?'

She grinned. She was good at hiding her feelings when she wanted to. 'I run an equal opportunities campaign group.'

'Terrific.'

He dumped the bag on the draining board, made the tea, and then leaned over her to look at the screen of the laptop as he handed her a mug. 'That's the list from Sky?'

'Yes. She says she's already checked it out for obvious phonies. There was only one name that didn't check out.' She held her breath. 'Yours. Apparently you're not a member of the National Union of Journalists.'

'I'm changing careers. My membership form's in the post.'

'And I'm the Queen of Sheba.'

He glanced sideways at her, his face just inches from her own. The creases at his eyes and mouth, the kind made by smiling, were close enough to count. She could almost feel the soft shadow of his five o'clock shadow grate against her skin.

It was unnerving to be this close to a man, to desire him not in her imagination but with her entire body, to want him in a way that was real, earthy and not in some fantasy dream-world.

He thought she was looking for a substitute for Gil, but he was wrong. Gil was a story-book hero, untouchable, unreachable. Matt was real; her mouth softened as she looked at him, her breasts felt heavy and there was an ache between her thighs...

She wanted him so much. And she wanted him now. She'd leave Sky to worry about Matt's hidden agenda. As for the rest...

'Do you have any immediate plans to tell me exactly who you are, Matt Crosby?'

He'd been waiting for the question. Had his answer all ready. 'Me? I'm nothing.' Only Nyssa mattered. That she was safe.

'You said that before. It isn't true. No one can ever be just...nothing.'

'You'd be surprised how easy it is.' He looked at the screen, tapped a key to scroll down the list. 'One day I had a great job in the City, lived in two thousand square feet of prime Docklands real estate and took three holidays a year in any exotic location that took my fancy. The next day...it was all gone.'

'That happened in one day? What did you do? Rob the Bank of England?'

'If I'd robbed the Bank of England I'd be some kind of folk hero, at least in the media.' His smile was genuine, if fleeting. 'What I did was far worse. I uncovered fraud in high places and I wasn't prepared to keep quiet about it while it was all tidied up, swept under the carpet. That made me dangerous, so I was neutralised. Overnight I became invisible. Nobody.'

'That's terrible.'

'Whistle-blowers win no prizes. I knew that. But you're right, of course; the process wasn't that swift. And it certainly wasn't pain-less. It was like being shot and then bleeding to death very slowly. It only takes a second to pull the trigger, but...'

'Hence the new career.'

His gaze, for a moment rock-steady, fal-tered, and he turned quickly away. 'I hope she didn't take offence at having her efficiency doubted,' he said. 'Sky?'

Nyssa forced herself to concentrate on the screen. 'No, of course not. She assumed Gil had offered to go through it for me. He's in the security business so he's got access to all kinds of information. She was sure he'd find out who you really are...' She ground to a halt, transfixed by his hands, by his long fin-gers as they worked at the keyboard

She clasped her hands tightly to prevent herself from reaching out to touch his grazed

and bruised knuckles. She reached out anyway, brushing her fingertips over the damage.
'Does it still hurt?' she asked.

He didn't answer, looked up. 'Not now,
Nyssa,' he said sharply. 'Not here. Please.' He
snatched back his hand, turned his back on her
and reached for his mug, his shoulders rigid
with the effort of keeping his distance.

So, despite his Galahad act, he felt the tug
of desire just as strongly as she did. She'd
thought he did, hoped he did, but this was all
so new to her that she couldn't be certain.
Until now. *Not now,* he'd said. *Not here.* Did
he think it would matter that it wasn't his
Docklands penthouse? Was it just pride?

Maybe, but his words were a promise that
he would make love to her, with her. Soon.
That he'd complete what had begun in that
moment when she'd looked around the
Assembly Rooms at Delvering and their gazes
had collided, held, locked…

She wanted to tell him that 'where' didn't
matter. It was 'who' that was important.
Already she'd learned that much. Instead she

said, 'I didn't tell Sky anything, Crosby. You asked me not to.'

'I wasn't sure you were listening.'

'I heard you.' But there was something that he wasn't telling her. He was hiding something, she knew, and a tiny shiver went through her. Doubt, for all her brave thoughts, was corrosive. 'But since you're about to collapse from hunger,' she said, slipping down from the stool and very firmly changing the subject, 'I suggest we leave this for now and start cooking.'

'We?'

She raised an eyebrow. 'You said you loved to cook.'

'Yes, but...'

'But?' she prompted, and when he didn't respond, continued, '*But* you were just pandering to the feminine need to nurture? *But* cooking is women's work and, being a man, you have a great many more important things to do?'

'Of course not. It's simply a question of priorities.' He didn't embarrass easily. 'Besides, it's really cramped in here. I thought you'd prefer to be left in peace—'

'While you relocate to the sofa and play detective with the laptop?' Nyssa picked up the bag of shallots he'd bought and pushed them into his hands. 'Your concern is noted. Now, start chopping, macho man.'

CHAPTER EIGHT

NYSSA thought he was going to argue, but after a moment he took the vegetables from her with a shrug that suggested she hadn't thought it through.

Working around one another in the little galley kitchen, getting under one another's feet, trying not to touch each other as they passed vegetables, pans, knives, compelled her to admit that Matt might have had a point.

But there was a reckless part of her that wanted him this close, wanted to tempt him to indiscretion, to provoke an unstoppable chain reaction. She was undoubtedly stupid beyond belief. Behaving in a manner that in anyone else would have had her throwing up her hands in despair at her stupidity.

Yet the truth was that she had never felt so alive. Her entire body was buzzing in the dangerous, touch-me-not atmosphere, and the rising temperature in the kitchen had little to do with cooking and everything to do with body heat.

It was, she thought, a bit like playing with matches. Reckless, foolish and you could so easily get burned... 'Have you got a wooden spoon?' she asked.

'I can't remember ever seeing one.'

'Have you ever looked?' He glanced up, then quickly looked away to open a drawer. There was one lying beneath a jumbled heap of kitchen cutlery and they both reached for it at the same time, their fingers colliding. Spoons, a fish slice, a carving fork clattered noisily to the floor.

Matt picked out the wooden spoon, rinsed it under the hot tap and then, holding it carefully by one end, offered it to her.

'Thanks.'

'You're welcome.'

The politeness was razor-edged with tension, but eventually the preparations were completed without anything more disastrous than a plate wobbling out of her fingers.

Matt cleared up the broken china without comment, although his rigid shoulders were practically screaming *I told you so*. She smiled to herself, and blew a kiss at his back before pouring olive oil into a pan and putting the vegetables to soften over the heat.

Stirring the mixture slowly, Nyssa glanced across at him as he dumped the broken pieces into the bin, and finally asked the question that had screamed at her from every corner of his flat.

'Are you divorced, Matt?'

'Good Lord, no.' She'd startled him out of his carefully maintained distance. 'Whatever made you ask that?'

'Lived with anyone?'

'Not recently.' He shrugged. 'Not here.'

'You didn't need to tell me that. This place has never had a woman's touch.' She glanced around, her gaze flickering quickly over the anonymous fixtures and fittings. 'How long have you been here?'

Matt concentrated on opening a bottle of wine he'd bought, even though it hadn't been on her list. 'A few months—a year, maybe. Why?'

Nyssa was sure he could have told her to the minute how long he'd lived there. And she was equally sure he hadn't meant that 'why' to slip out, giving her an opening. She took it mercilessly. 'Well, you haven't taken much effort to make it comfortable, have you? In fact you might have moved in yesterday for all the impression you've made on it.'

'Maybe I just don't get a buzz from co-ordinating soft furnishings.'

'Maybe not, but what about photographs, a decent sound system, a pile of your favourite videos?'

'You've already pointed out that I don't have a television.'

'You know what I mean. This place is about as homey as a dentist's waiting room.' She shook her head. 'No, it's worse. A dentist leaves a few magazines about to brighten the place up.'

'I seem to have bypassed the excitement of browsing through magazines. Have I missed much?'

'I'd have thought they'd be basic research tools for a man in your line of work.' As much as she'd tried to ignore Sky's note, it had awakened her curiosity. She hadn't, she thought, been anywhere near curious enough about her mysterious knight errant. Or maybe she hadn't wanted to enquire too deeply in case she didn't like what she heard. He'd come up with a pretty convincing reason for his lack of journalistic credentials, but she wanted more. Much more. 'It looks like the temporary home of a man who's been stripped of everything he's ever possessed by an asset-stripping ex-wife.'

'The mortgage was pulled on my apartment. Part of the treatment. I had a choice to make. Sell my home, or sell my soul. I didn't want to bring any of that life with me.'

'But there's not a single thing that's *personal*. There isn't even the usual stack of junk mail, for heaven's sake.'

'Junk mail goes where it belongs. In the bin. Unopened. Am I making a mistake?'

'Probably not.' She didn't look at him, but concentrated on the vegetables. 'Not since your idea of light reading appears to consist of a treatise on investment law or banking history. Or fraud.' She glanced at him, thought about the filing cabinet hidden in a cupboard and bolted to the floor. 'Are you still hoping to expose them?'

'I suffer from insomnia. Those books are more effective than anything prescribed by a doctor. Pass me a couple of glasses from that cupboard, will you?' She reached up, hesitated. 'On the other hand, maybe it would be safer if I did it.'

He reached over her head, not quite touching her, but the movement was close enough to stir her hair and her skin shivered as if he'd stroked her.

She watched him pour the wine, his hand rock-steady. Maybe she was wrong. Maybe he wasn't getting the same reaction from their closeness... 'That would explain your clothes, then,' she said. Anything to distract her from the thickness of his wrist, the way the light caught and shone on the hair of his forearm. She'd bet he played tennis like a champion.

'My clothes?' She jerked herself out of the fantasy her mind was running and realised that he was looking down at the jeans he was wearing. 'They're scarcely worth a mention.'

'I was referring to all those beautifully tailored business suits in plastic covers hanging up in your wardrobe.' She added the rice to the pan, then glanced at him. 'I was pretty sure that hack journalists don't wear chalkstripe.' She wasn't expecting an answer so she didn't wait for one. 'Or handmade shoes. Or shirts with Jermyn Street labels.'

'You *have* been making yourself at home.'

'Making myself useful. I shook out your dinner jacket—it was covered in sand and could do with a trip to the dry cleaners, by the way—and hung it up along with the clothes I brought with me.'

'Was there enough room? From the weight of your bag, I imagine you brought an entire wardrobe of instant disguises with you.'

'Since you won't let me go back to my own place, I had to improvise. There are some places a little black dress simply will not take a girl. Much like a chalk-stripe suit.' She flashed him a smile.

'Was there some point to this conversation?' he asked, not much amused.

'No.' She added a little liquid to the saucepan; it steamed and sizzled noisily. When it quieted down, she carried on. 'I just wouldn't want you to think I had been entirely taken in by your adopted persona, Crosby.'

'It's just as well I came clean, then.'

'Did you? Entirely? You asked me to trust you, and against all the evidence—and until I'm proved wrong—I'm inclined to believe you have my best interests at heart. That's about as far as I'm prepared to go.'

'Thank you.'

'You're welcome.' She reached out, took the glass from his hand and clinked it against his. 'Cheers.' He remained silent. 'This is going to take a little while, but it only needs one of us. Why don't you go on through to the living room and check out Sky's list?'

Nyssa continued to stir the risotto, carefully adding small quantities of the liquid and, Matt thought, just as carefully avoiding looking at him. He, on the other hand, couldn't take his eyes off her wrist as it turned the spoon. Her economy of movement, the stillness of every other part of her, caught at his heart, kept him pinned to the spot.

After a while she glanced sideways at him. 'I thought you had a hot date with a laptop.'

'It'll keep.' He and the laptop had all night to get cosy; he wasn't going to be getting any quality sleep on that sofa. 'Right now I'm deriving pleasure from the unexpected sight of you getting domestic.'

She raised her expressive brows a fraction. 'You don't get out much, do you?'

'This has been an exceptional week,' he admitted. 'And I still have ahead of me the doubtful pleasure of breaking into a derelict cinema.'

'It isn't derelict. And you volunteered to be my minder,' she reminded him.

'I must be crazy.'

'I'm hoping that's the reason.' She looked at him again, her blue eyes suddenly thoughtful.

'You can count on it,' he said.

'Then relax, we're not breaking in to the cinema, or anywhere else.' She continued to add liquid to the rice.

'How do you propose to get inside?' he asked, when she left it at that.

'We're going to walk up to the security guard and ask him, very nicely, to let us in.'

'We're both crazy.'

'Not at all. You and your chalk-stripe suit are going to prove very useful. You'll look like a prosperous businessman. Who will dare question your authority?' She smiled, every bit like a cat that had got at the cream. 'Hmm?'

'Forget the chalk-stripe. That's City wear.'

'Is it?' She glanced sideways at him. 'Pity.'

'Tell me, when I use my one telephone call, who shall I ring to bail us out?'

'It isn't going to happen.' She grinned. 'Trust me,' she said. Yes, well, he probably deserved that one. 'And, if it does all go pear-shaped…'

'Yes?'

'I'll ask if we can share a cell and you can pass the time by telling me the whole story of your fall from favour. I have the feeling that might just be worth getting arrested for.'

'I'd advise you to wait for the movie.'

'Ah, but will there be a cinema in Delvering to screen it?'

It was time to move before his stupid mouth got him into trouble…more trouble than he was already in. 'How long will that be?' he asked, nodding in the direction of the pan.

'Twenty-five minutes—' she waggled her free hand '—or thereabouts. If you're staying you might as well start grating that parmesan.'

'I'll pass, thanks. Can I take this?' He didn't wait for an answer but picked up her laptop, retreated to the living room and, while he booted up his own, more powerful machine, retrieved Sky's e-mail from the 'trash' bin. He wanted to know exactly what she'd said about him.

Not much. Just that if he was a journalist, he was a singularly unsuccessful one but that probably Gil could find out more. So Nyssa still didn't know anything about his dealings with Parker.

It didn't take long to check out the *bona fides* of the people who'd come to the meeting. The genuine journalists were easily excluded; the internet instantly threw up stories they'd written in the past two or three years. That was why he'd been so simple to spot as a fake. He hadn't had time to set up that kind of cover; but then he hadn't anticipated the necessity.

The public officials and other interested parties didn't take much longer to cross off the list of possible suspects. They were real people living ordinary lives. Everyone checked out. Which meant just one thing. The four names he was looking for weren't on the list.

'It's ready.' Nyssa looked around the door. 'Oh, bless. His-and-hers laptops. Are they net-working?'

He made no comment, simply moved them out of the way in silence, and while she set the plates on the coffee table he fetched the wine and refilled their glasses, before picking up a plate and retreating to the safety of an armchair made for one. It wasn't particularly comfortable, the springing was of the random variety, but it was a lot safer than sharing the sofa with Nyssa in her present mood.

'This is good,' he said, after taking a mouthful of the risotto.

'Then why are you frowning?'

'Was I? It wasn't anything to do with the food, I promise.'

A fork halfway to her mouth, she paused. 'Have you found something?'

'No. Everyone checked out.' Which wasn't as reassuring as it sounded. 'I was thinking,' he said, before she could work that out for herself. 'What your campaign needs is a celebrity to go into bat for you, someone to catch the public's imagination. Do you suppose Doris Catchpole, star of the silver screen, could still be with us?'

'Doris Catchpole?' she repeated. 'Don't be silly, you made her up.'

'Only the name. I'm willing to bet that back in the golden age of cinema some glamorous starlet got her picture in all the papers when she opened Delvering's wonderful new picture palace.'

Nyssa frowned. 'Sky's got all the research files, but I do recall a photograph of someone in a slinky dress...' Then she shook her head. 'She'd have to be ninety at least.'

'It's a long shot, I know, but worth checking out. If she's still alive she might enjoy a chance to relive her glory days, or find a publisher for a ghostwritten memoir. If she became really famous that might be enough.'

'Brains as well as brawn. I love it.' She left him to deal with the plates while she set to work, hunting down information on the web.

He returned to find her staring at the screen in disbelief.

'What is it?'

'Meet Doris Catchpole.'

He glanced at the screen. 'Good grief, that looks like...' He stopped because it plainly couldn't be.

'It's Kitty's great-aunt. She was quite a star in her day.'

'But that's...' He was going to say terrific, but stopped himself just in time.

'It's a pity. She's the one person in the world I couldn't possibly expect to help me. The one person I couldn't ask.'

He thought she was wrong. He thought that Kitty would do anything in the world to make Nyssa happy—short of divorcing her husband.

The cinema at the centre of all the fuss was boarded up, fly-posted and, from the café on the far side of the road, didn't look much like an architectural gem in need of saving for the nation. In fact the whole area was run down, and Matt said so.

'And you think a supermarket will improve things?' She put down her cup and leaned across the table. 'See that newsagent? That will be the first to go. Then this place, then the greengrocer. The supermarket will kill off all the small businesses in the area. The cinema, if it's restored, will revitalise the area. It's happened in other places.'

'I'm sure you've done your homework.' He finished his coffee. 'It's smaller than I expected.'

'Too small for the multi-screens to be interested, but it'll make a perfect arthouse cinema.' Nyssa's face glowed with enthusiasm. 'Have you seen the pictures of the inside, when it was new?'

'I saw some at your presentation, but surely it's all fallen to pieces? The place has been everything but well cared for in the last few years.'

'That's what Charles Parker wants everyone to believe: that there's nothing worth conserving. So why hasn't he knocked it down?' When he didn't answer, she said, 'Shall we go and find out?' She began to rise, but he put his hand on her arm, restraining her.

'No, stay here. Let's see if the security guard accepts that card at face value before you get involved.' He glanced down at the slender-heeled shoes she was wearing to go with the distracting sex-kitten image she'd adopted as her persona for the morning. Shoes that displayed her feet and ankles to perfection. 'You won't be able to run very fast in those. Or in that skirt.'

She grinned. 'I'd kick them off and hike my skirt up if I had to run.'

'Then you're definitely staying here. I'm not prepared to be responsible for a major traffic pile-up.'

'My hero.'

Not exactly. He had a very good reason for not wanting Nyssa with him as he crossed the road and approached the security guard's hut.

'My name's Crosby,' he said. 'I'm a security consultant for Charles Parker.' He gave the man his own card instead of the one Nyssa had produced from a large collection she kept for use in such circumstances.

The guard put the card by the phone and pushed the visitor's book towards him. 'No one will get in here,' he said. 'This place is locked up tight as the Tower of London.'

'Then we'll need the keys,' Matt said gravely, as he signed the book.

He grinned. 'Yeah, right. I'll just have to call the office to check, then I'll show you around,' he said enthusiastically. 'It's an amazing place. You wouldn't believe...' He was beginning to get the idea, Matt thought, as the man put through a call to Parker's office, then held out the phone to him. 'Mr Parker would like a word, sir.'

Aware that Nyssa was watching him from the safety of the café, Matt ignored it. 'Tell him I'll ring him later. When I've completed my report.'

The guard blenched, but relayed the message, then said, 'You'll have to wear a hard hat. Health and Safety.'

He wasn't arguing; the place was undoubtedly falling to pieces. 'Make that two. I have my assistant with me. If she ever finishes her coffee.' He turned and gave Nyssa a hurry-up wave—every inch the impatient businessman.

Nyssa, looking like the kind of PA every man had ever dreamed about, teasingly took her own sweet time in sauntering across the road, clearly intent on proving a point.

The security guard couldn't take his eyes off her, and Matt was convinced he must see through the curly blonde wig, the grey contacts she was wearing to tone down her vivid eyes.

He'd have known her anywhere. But though she walked right up to the man, flashing him a blazing smile as she took the safety helmet, the poor bloke was too busy admiring her accentuated cleavage to connect her with the troublesome Miss Blake.

They donned the white hard hats emblazoned with Parker's logo as they were let in through a side door. 'You'll want all the lights, I expect?'

'Give me everything you've got.' Gradually the lights came on all over the building, illuminating the foyer, the stairs and curving mezzanine floor, cantilevered above them. Matt had expected broken light fixtures, dirt, rubbish, the cobwebs of ages, but there was only a film of dust to dull the old magic. Beside him Nyssa gasped, and she was right. The rundown exterior belied the inside of the building. It was a long way from derelict.

'Do you want me to show you where everything is?'

'What? Oh, no, we'll find our own way round—' he glanced at the man's identity badge '—Gary. You don't want any of that Save the Gaumont crowd sneaking in while your back's turned, do you?'

'You were born to this, Matt,' Nyssa said, when the security guard had gone.

'I have the uneasy feeling you mean that to be a compliment.'

But she was too busy looking around to respond. 'Would you say this has all been cleaned up pretty recently?'

'I guess so. Is that a problem?' He'd have thought she'd be pleased, but she looked concerned.

'Parker's plans don't involve restoration.'

'I'm sure he hasn't gone to all this trouble just to rip it out and dump it in a skip.'

'No. More likely to ship it to America, or Japan, or Germany, where it will be appreciated. This has been done so prospective buyers can see what they're bidding for.'

'Is there really much of a market for this stuff?'

'Are you kidding?' She turned back to him when he didn't immediately respond. 'There's a huge market for art deco interiors, but this was designed all of a piece. Once it's split up, it's lost. Here it's…well, it's perfect.'

'Why don't you give me the guided tour?'

She needed no second invitation, but grabbed his hand and set off in the direction of the elegant sweeping staircase. At the foot she stopped, took out a handkerchief and wiped the light film of dust from the black and gold figure of an Ankara dancer holding a lamp aloft. 'Isn't she beautiful?'

'Stunning,' he said.

'The whole interior is special, Matt. Unique.'

'What's up there?' he asked.

'Come and see.' She ran up the stairs and held her arms wide as she spun around. 'At one time this was *the* place in Delvering to take afternoon tea. Silver teapots, cucumber sandwiches, exquisite fancies, and waitresses in black dresses with white lace aprons and caps. Just look at those wall lamps!' She groaned. 'He's going to rip the heart out of this building, isn't he? Sell it off bit by bit to collectors unless we stop him.'

It certainly explained why Parker hadn't saved himself a lot of trouble by simply bull-dozing the lot months ago. 'And through there?'

'The balcony seats.'

He pushed open one of the polished swing doors and she followed him into an auditorium fitted out in the art deco Egyptian style favoured by big cinema chains in the thirties. It made the modern multi-screens look very ordinary. 'I can see how you might get caught up in the magic,' he said.

'There aren't many places left like this. It's part of twentieth-century history.'

Taking the handkerchief from her, he brushed the dust off a couple of plush tip-up seats from which the gilt had long been rubbed.

'Would you care to step back in time and join me in the back row, ma'am?'

'For a history lesson?'

His mouth was a mile ahead of his brain. Or maybe he was just kidding himself. 'It may be the last chance you'll get.'

She pulled a face. 'Not if I can help it.' Then, with a saucy grin. 'Will you buy me a choc ice?'

'The minute the girl with the tray walks by,' he promised, and, taking off his hard hat, handed her into the seat. Then he sat down beside her, running his arm along the back of the seats, so that it just touched her shoulders.

The security guard wasn't alone in his fascination with the way her suit was cut to display her curves.

'What we need now is the Wurlitzer organ to rise and fill the place with music.' Her voice caught in her throat as he removed the hard hat she was wearing. 'What's showing?'

'This is fantasy. It can be anything you want.'

'Something really glamorous,' she said quickly, looking anywhere but at him. 'What about Fred Astaire in *Top Hat*? Wouldn't that be perfect? Or one of those Bette Davis movies, cool and sophisticated but with simmering undercurrents of passion beneath the surface.'

Forget the screen. There were plenty of dangerous undercurrents right here in the auditorium, he thought, and when he didn't answer, she finally looked up at him, her head tilted back, unconsciously seductive, her mouth as red and inviting as a ripe strawberry. Despite the grey contacts her eyes were burning hot and bright beneath a silky fringe of lashes.

'What about you?' she asked.

'What about me?'

She swallowed, as if she realised that it was vital to keep talking but wasn't entirely sure why. 'What movie would you like to see?'

His mouth wasn't the only part of him running ahead of common sense. His arm was fast catching up, slipping down the seat until his hand was resting against her neck, his fingers against her warm skin. This had been a bad idea. He should move. Only his fingers obeyed the thought, teasing along the sensitive edge of her backbone. Beneath his hand, her body seemed to melt.

'No one who sat here ever came to see the movie,' he murmured.

'Is that right?' Her voice was little more than a whisper. 'This is all just…history to me.'

'I'm pretty good at history. Shall I tell you how it goes?'

She raised a finger to his mouth, tugging at his lower lip. 'Did anyone ever tell you that you talk too much, Crosby? Just do it.'

The invitation was a sweet mixture of knowing boldness and uncertainty. Here was danger touched with the edgy excitement of the new: a step into the void. And not just for her. This had all the hallmarks of a life-changing moment, and, feeling a lot like a sixteen-year-old on his first hot date, Matt lowered his mouth to her lips, brushing against them, touching them softly.

He'd offered her fantasy. It was all he had to give and he was determined that it should be memorable. And not just for her. He had a fantasy of his own, a desire to leave an indelible imprint, a memory so strong that whenever she went to the movies for the rest of her life, whoever she was with, she would remember him.

Her arms encircled his neck and beneath him she mewed softly as she parted her lips for him, her tongue, her entire body reaching for him, soft and yielding, all woman. He was definitely kidding himself. He was building memories for himself. And he was the one who would never forget.

Kissing Matt Crosby was an experience that simply got better, Nyssa discovered, as if he'd taken note of every touch, her every sigh, and stored it up so that each time he could take her somewhere new, show her some different delight. He was so gentle, so tender, so very thorough…

Or maybe she was the one who was on a learning curve so steep that it was taking her breath away. She had never realised that a simple kiss could set her whole body on fire, make it yearn for something unimaginable. She whimpered as she ached for more, ached to be touched, held, loved, and then, quite unexpectedly, discovered the need not just to take, but to give Matt everything his heart desired.

But then this wasn't a simple kiss. It was complex and deep and searching as his tongue stroked against hers. His fingers had tangled in her hair as he held her and she hated the wig she was wearing for getting in the way. She wanted to feel his fingers against her scalp, against her skin, his body against hers.

As if he could read her mind, he began to unfasten the buttons of her jacket, letting cooler air seep against her skin, goosing it, setting it on edge. And then his hand cradled her breast through thin silk, his thumb teasing a sharp and demanding response. This was better, this was real, and she knew, beyond all shadow of a doubt, that she wanted to be naked in his arms, to be possessed, to belong to him alone.

Even as the begging words formed in her head, as she began to slither down against him, intent on carrying through her dream, he stopped her, holding her head between his hands so that he could look straight into her eyes.

His own were all question, demanding to know if the fantasy was living up to its billing. As she clung to him for support she had only one coherent thought.

Don't stop. Please don't stop.

CHAPTER NINE

'NYSSA?' She bit her lip to stop the words she knew he didn't want to hear. 'Are you all right?'

'Fine,' she managed. 'Great. You're a terrific teacher. History is now absolutely my favourite subject.'

His hand cradled her cheek as he pulled her close. 'Then why are you crying?' he murmured.

'Crying?'

He brushed her cheek with his thumb and pressed it to her mouth. It was wet, salty against her lips as she touched it with her tongue. Well, tears were about right. She wanted to weep. Wanted to thank him for that night at Delvering when she'd thrown herself at him and he'd had the strength of character to say no. And again at James's party.

She'd been looking for a quick fix, someone to save her from herself, wipe out hopeless dreams, and anyone without his moral scruples would have gone ahead without a thought for how she'd feel afterwards. But Matt Crosby was different from most men. She'd known it instinctively, and even though she'd taxed him cruelly he'd made her wait until she was certain. Well, she was certain. She wanted him more than any man alive on earth. Bar none.

But he was right. The back row of the stalls was not the place. They weren't history, they were brand-new, with a whole new life waiting for them. Tonight they would be staying at the Delvering Arms and that was the proper place to begin.

'Crying?' She pulled herself together, blinked a little, dashed the tears away with her shaking fingers. 'I'm not crying,' she said. 'That's just the dust getting to my contacts and making my eyes water.'

'Then maybe we should finish the tour and check the doors so the guard doesn't get suspicious.' He kissed her again, but gently this time, before taking out a clean handkerchief to replace the one she'd used as a duster and carefully blotting her cheeks before handing it to her to finish the job.

'Okay,' she said, her voice still trembly despite her best efforts. 'But you still owe me a choc ice.'

'We'll come back when the cinema's restored to its former glory. I'll reserve these two seats for the opening night.'

'You really think we can do it?'

'I believe you can do anything you set your mind to.' For a moment his gaze continued to hold hers with a look that had her heart skipping with any number of here-and-now possibilities... Then he bent to retrieve their helmets from the floor. 'Okay?' he said, placing one firmly back on her head.

'It's a date,' she confirmed, and stood up quickly while her legs remained hers to command, but as she moved to push past him he caught her shoulder, stopping her, turning her to face him.

'Rule Number One for the back row of the cinema, sweetheart. Check your clothing before leaving your seat.' Then, with a look that made her regret the speed at which she'd moved, he cupped the soft mounds of her breasts in his hands and bent to place a light kiss between them, a pledge of more to come, before he refastened the buttons of her jacket. 'We wouldn't want the guard to think we were doing anything more exciting than checking out the security systems, would we?'

She opened her mouth to agree with him, but the word didn't materialise. He looked up. She cleared her throat. 'No.'

'Have you seen everything?'

'No. There's another floor, but I'm not sure where the stairs are.' She took the briefcase he was carrying, took out the plans and spread them out over the back of the seats.

'It looks like living accommodation.'

'It was the manager's flat back in the days when he wore a dinner jacket in the evening. I wonder if it's still got the original fittings?'

'I doubt it. It probably had a 1950s makeover. The latest thing in red Formica.'

'Maybe, but it's worth a look. I may not get another chance.' She took a digital camera from the briefcase, then glanced at her wristwatch. 'We're running out of time. Why don't you go and rattle the doors to make it look good, while I take some photographs?'

'There's no hurry.' He grinned. 'As highly paid consultants we have to look at every aspect of security, and that takes time.' He gathered up the plans. 'We'll do it together.'

Matt drove to the rear of the Delvering Arms while Nyssa divested herself of the wig and contact lenses. They collected the keys of the rooms he'd booked earlier by phone and retrieved Nyssa's bag from the porter. 'What now?' he asked, as they made their way upstairs.

'Rinse off the dust and change into something more comfortable,' she offered.

'Right.' Changing into something more comfortable had a lot to commend it. For more than a year all he'd wanted to do was to get back into a suit and resume his life at the point where it had been so abruptly halted. It occurred to him, as he climbed the stairs, loosening his tie as he went, that somewhere between first setting eyes on Nyssa Blake and now not only his priorities but his entire world had changed.

'And I'd better give Sky a call. We've got to set up a rota to keep watch in case Parker tries to dismantle the place and ship out the interiors. Can you download these photographs onto the computer while I change? I want to send them to English Heritage and the Department of the Environment, whip them into action. What I really could do with is a website. Pete is the man for that—'

He slowed. 'Who's Pete?'

'Don't look like that, Matt. I've known Pete for years…'

'And you've only known me for days. I know. But I'm the one who's supposed to be taking care of you.'

'Well, you build the website, then.'

'You think I can't?'

'No, but—'

'Just tell me what you want and I'll organise a website for you. But you've got to stay here while I do it.'

'Sure? Well, okay, then. Except—' He stopped and slowly turned to face her, and she raised both hands, palms out to him, as if fending off anticipated wrath. 'No! Don't look at me like that. It's just the planning committee meeting. It's only next door in the Town Hall. I'll be quite safe...' Her smile was as bright as a toothpaste ad, and about as convincing.

'You know, sweetheart,' he said, with a drawl that in no way disguised his very real anger at her reckless disregard for her own safety, 'I've just had a really great idea.'

'What? No, you can't come with me. I need that webpage—'

'I'll kidnap you myself.'

She laughed. Then, as the smile faded from her lips and something in her expression shifted, the atmosphere in the dim upstairs

hallway of the centuries-old inn changed sub-
tly. 'That's not a good plan, Matt.'

'Any plan that keeps you safe is a good
plan.'

'But what about you?' Her voice was even,
reasonable, but her eyes sparkled back at him
with a flash of rebellion so vivid that he
caught his breath.

This wasn't the girl who'd trembled in his
arms, who'd cried when he kissed her, but a
jolting reminder that Nyssa Blake was capable
of badly shaking a bully like Charles Parker,
that she was a woman who could make poli-
ticians think again. Her private life might have
been filled with pain, but in the public arena
she knew exactly what she wanted and would
stop at nothing to get it. Even if it meant putting herself in danger.

'What about me?' he asked.

'How safe will you be?' She didn't wait for
his answer. 'Think about it,' she said. 'Would
you tie me up, for instance?'

He'd simply been making a point, as well
she knew. 'Don't be foolish, Nyssa.'

'I think you'd have to,' she said, with the utmost seriousness, 'because I'd definitely try to escape.' She lifted her hands, wrists together, and held them out in front of her for a moment, before apparently changing her mind. 'No, that's too easy. I could undo the knots with my teeth. Behind my back would be best. Of course you'd have to feed me, wash me, do everything for me... You wouldn't be able to take your eyes off me for a moment...' She paused, and this time her smile was teasing. 'Are you thinking about it?' she asked. 'Could you handle it?'

He caught her wrists in one of his hands. Held them tight. 'I'll do whatever I have to,' he said fiercely. 'Don't believe for a second that I won't. I don't want anything bad to happen to you. Can't you understand that? I—' He bit off the words.

'You what, Crosby?' Her voice was soft as eiderdown.

'I wish you wouldn't call me that,' he said abruptly, then dropped her hands and turned to check the numbers on the doors. He opened one and stood back. 'I'll see you in a few minutes,' he said, and, turning on his heel, walked swiftly on to the next door.

Nyssa, fired up on a mixture of anger at Matt's high-handedness and go-to-hell desire provoked by her own imagery, ignored the room he'd chosen for her. Instead she followed him, watched him fit the key in the lock. As he bent to pick up his bag and toss it into the room he noticed that she was standing at his side.

'What?' he asked. 'What's the matter?'

'Nothing. I'd just prefer this room.'

He shrugged. 'They're exactly the same.'

'No, Matt. You're in this one.' She let her bag drop from her shoulder and closed in on him, backing him into the room, kicking the door shut behind her. Then she grabbed the lapels of his jacket and pulled him down until his face was inches from her own. 'And you're right. If you're to keep me safe, you should be at my side. Day and night.'

He swallowed. 'I'm glad you've finally got the message, but—'

'There's something else.'

'What?'

'I still owe you a shower.' Then she kissed him hard, giving the words plenty of time to sink in, before she eased her grip and leaned back to meet his gaze head-on.

'Now?' His expression was totally dispassionate. 'I thought you had a meeting to attend.' He was so-o-o cool. But his eyes weren't cool. He wasn't fooling her for a minute.

'I have. But I'm keeping tonight free. Make a note in your diary.' Then she smiled. 'And in case you're wondering why I'm telling you in advance—' she waited, but he didn't have anything pressing to say '—it's because once in while I like to know what you're thinking. This way I'll know exactly what's on your mind between now and then. Right?'

'You've got it,' he said, with every appearance of struggling for his breath. Nyssa had some sympathy with him; it hadn't been a piece of cake for her to let him go. But so far she'd been doing all the chasing, while her knight errant had been doing all the stepping back, saying no even when his eyes were saying yes, yes, yes... It was time for a little of that direct action that she was so famous for.

'Well, good,' she said. 'I'm glad that's settled.' And for the first time in days she felt strong again, back in the driving seat. But just to make sure he'd got the message she unbuttoned her jacket and let it drop to the floor. Then she unzipped her skirt and let it slither over her hips before stepping out of it. He didn't move, and as she unzipped her bag she looked up. 'You don't mind if I go first in the bathroom?'

He made the slightest gesture that suggested she should help herself. Then, with a disquieting little smile that lifted just one corner of his mouth and a look that scanned the length of her body, so that her mouth dried and her breath caught in her throat, he said, 'Since it's a date, I think I should buy you dinner...first.' There was the merest pause between the words 'dinner' and 'first'. A pause that rang like a bass bell. 'What do you think? A little candlelight and champagne to set the mood?'

She swallowed. 'Whatever you think.'

'I think…' His face remained impassive. 'I think we'd better order room service.'

So much for taking control. Two seconds was all it had taken him to regain the initiative.

With a squeak that might have been 'great', she grabbed her clothes and dived for the safety of the bathroom, leaning back against the door to stare at her reflection in the heavy gilt mirror. This was the image she'd intended Matt Crosby to carry in his head for the rest of the day: the black silk teddy, the long suspenders holding up gossamer-thin black stockings and the high, high heels.

Then she groaned. As a passion-dampening counterpoint to the seductive lingerie, her cheeks were flushed so red that they clashed with her hair.

It had taken all her courage to put on that sexy lady show, and all the time her colouring had been giving her away. He was probably killing himself with laughter right now.

Matt listened to the water splashing in the sink and would have gambled on his life that it was cold. Not that Nyssa's bold self-assertion had been in any way undermined by the hot flush of her cheeks. If anything, the blush that betrayed her innocence only served to fuel the hot desire that he'd fought so hard to keep under control for days but which was, at this moment, in imminent danger of consuming him.

He tore off his jacket and tossed it on the bed before crossing to the window and flinging it open, desperate for air. It wasn't much help. The day was hot and the faint breeze was woefully inadequate to cool the fire Nyssa had generated deep within him.

He had to tell her. He had to tell her everything now, while she could still tell him to go to hell. He'd have to take that risk, because there was no way he was making love to her with a lie on his lips. And he couldn't reject her again. She would never understand, never believe in a million years that he was only protecting her from making a big mistake. And maybe she'd be right. Maybe he was just thinking of himself.

But as he clung to the sill, fighting the urge to follow her into the bathroom and make that a cold shower for two, he saw something in the street below that cooled him off faster, and more effectively, than a bucket of ice water.

He didn't stop to change, just grabbed his jacket, and the camera, and headed for the door, hammering on the bathroom door as he passed. 'Nyssa, stay where you are. Don't answer the door to anyone. No room service. Nothing.'

'What?' She flung open the bathroom door, her hair sticking damply about her face, still in that mind-blowing underwear. 'What's up? Where are you going?' For a moment he was tempted to simply bundle her up and carry her off himself, as he'd threatened. Keep her somewhere safe where no one would ever find them. 'Matt?'

'I've just spotted one of those thugs from the other night.'

'What? Where?'

'Down in the street.' She made a move towards the window, but he caught her hands, holding her against him. 'Stay here.'

'While you go after him on your own? Are you crazy?' She turned to reach for her trousers. 'I'm coming with you.'

'No.' And, when she would have protested, he covered her mouth briefly with his own. Then repeated, 'No. I just want to see where he goes. Who he sees. But I can't do that unless I know you're safe. I want you to stay here, with the door locked, until I get back. Promise?' She gave a little shrug that might have meant anything, but when he continued to wait she finally nodded. 'Thank you.'

'But what about the planning meeting? I made some objections and I want to know what happens.'

'Read about it in the evening newspaper, the same as everyone else.'

*   *   *

Matt paused within the shadows of the hotel entrance to scan the far side of the road, mentally calculating the distance the man would have travelled while he was arguing with Nyssa.

For a moment he thought he'd taken too long to explain, that he'd lost his quarry. Then, glancing back, he saw him. He'd stopped a few yards shy of the hotel and was deep in conversation with a woman in a smart black suit, hair neatly coiled at her nape, a briefcase at her side. She half turned to gesture towards the hotel, and as the sun lit up her face he raised the camera to capture the image in the hopes that he could identify her. With her face isolated and enlarged in the viewfinder, he realised that it wasn't going to be a problem.

With a sinking heart he discovered he wasn't anywhere near as surprised as he should have been to see that it was Sky.

Nyssa paced anxiously back and forth across the bedroom floor, stopping only to peer out

of the window every few seconds, calling herself every kind of fool since Matt left.

It had been madness to let him go after the
man on his own. Suppose he was recognised?
Kidnapping was a serious crime; anyone
who'd even consider it had to be capable of
almost anything. Her stomach lurched sick-
eningly at the thought of him lying hurt somewhere, bleeding, needing help... She glanced
at the phone. Gil would know what to do...

The sudden rap at the door made her jump
like a nervous kitten. This was it. This was
someone coming to take her to the hospital...
Someone coming to tell her that he was hurt.
Worse—

'Nyssa? Are you there?'

She let out a sigh of relief and ran to the
door, flinging it open. 'Sky.' Then, 'Good
grief.'

'You're not the only one who can dress to
confuse. I've just been to the planning meeting and, dressed like this, no one gave me a
second glance.' She dropped her briefcase and
flung herself into a chair. 'Your disguise must

have been very good,' she said dryly. 'I didn't spot you there. Or maybe you had something more important to do?'

Nyssa brushed aside Sky's snide remarks. 'What happened?'

'Well, it's good news. The objections you raised have been noted and the Highways Department have got involved. Parker's been told to go back to the drawing board and re-submit a new design which includes two hundred parking spaces.' She grinned. 'Now we've got time to rally the troops and make our presence really felt. I thought a demo on Saturday morning—'

'For heaven's sake, Sky, act your age. We don't need your hooligans causing havoc in the town centre, upsetting everyone. What we need is the establishment on our side. Even if the planning application for redevelopment is thrown out, we still have to save the cinema. It will take a lot of money.' In truth, she was a lot less worried about the cinema at that moment than what Matt was doing, whether he was safe, and she crossed to the window again, checked her watch for the hundredth time. He'd been gone more than an hour. He had to be in trouble or he'd have rung her…

She turned, and saw Sky staring at her.

'What on earth is the matter with you?'

'Sorry,' Nyssa said, with a gesture intended to brush away the worry. 'I didn't mean to snap.' She took a deep breath. 'Actually, I've been busy, too. I got into the cinema this morning and it's good news on that front as well,' she said, with determined briskness. 'Parker's done us a big favour by cleaning the place up. He's made it a lot easier to convince English Heritage that the place needs listing. I've got photographs…' She looked around to show her the snaps and realised the camera had gone. 'Bother. Matt must have taken the camera.'

'Matt?' Sky enquired softly. 'Matt Crosby?'

Nyssa flushed. 'Well, yes.'

'But I warned you…' Sky's gaze suddenly focused on the two bags side by side on the bed. 'Oh, for heaven's sake! You are such a little idiot! I told you he didn't check out.'

'I know, but—'

'I suppose he was with you when you opened my e-mail, whispering sweet nothings in your shell-like ear?'

'I'm sorry?' Nyssa was used to hiding her feelings, and she hid them now beneath a puzzled smile.

'Oh, don't play the innocent with me. I can see what he's done to you. It's right there in your eyes. With all the men in the world to choose from...' Sky threw up her hands in despair. 'I suppose it was only a matter of time. You must have been a walking time bomb, and that man could light anyone's fuse—'

'Your point being?' Nyssa asked coldly.

'What have you told him?'

'I told him he hadn't passed your credibility check.'

'And I've no doubt he had some very convincing story to explain that?'

Nyssa, who'd so far been too annoyed by her aide's unpleasant reaction to consider why she might be so mad, stilled. Matt's story had been short on detail, but it didn't matter because she trusted him. Believed that he cared. And that was enough.

'He convinced me,' she said.

'Your innocence does you credit.' Maybe she was ultra-sensitive on the subject, but to Nyssa her lieutenant's sympathetic smile didn't seem to entirely match her words. 'However misplaced.'

'I think I'm the best judge of that.'

'Do you? Really? Well, let me tell you something. We've got a new recruit, someone on the inside, who's fallen in love with the Gaumont and, like us, would do anything to save it—'

'Not anything,' she responded sharply. Nyssa suspected that, for all her gentle flower child image, Sky thrived on confrontation, and was impatient at her meetings with those whom she considered the enemy. 'We raise the banner and make the case—then it's for the people of Delvering to choose. They've got to want it or the Gaumont has no future.' Sky made no comment, simply shrugged. 'So, who is this new recruit of yours? What's he told you?'

'He's the security guard at the site. And he's told me that your precious Matt Crosby is Charles Parker's man.'

CHAPTER TEN

'MATT works for Charles Parker?' Nyssa didn't need Sky's look of barely concealed triumph to tell her that it was so. It all fell into place so neatly. For heaven's sake her first thought when she had met Matt had been that he was all part of the act. 'How does the security guard know for sure?'

'Crosby turned up at the site this morning with some bimbo in tow. Apparently he's Parker's "security consultant".' She was making little quote marks with her fingers when it apparently occurred to her who the 'bimbo' must have been. 'Oh—'

Nyssa gestured impatiently. 'Go on.'

'The security staff always double-check with the office before they let anyone on the site. When our man rang in about Crosby, Parker himself came on the line, wanting to speak to him.'

'But I was watching him from...' From across the road. Where he'd insisted she stay. 'Matt didn't speak to anyone,' she continued. It was somehow vital that Sky shouldn't see that she doubted him.

'No. He said he'd call Parker later. When he'd completed his report. Apparently Parker took it like a lamb.'

'How did your man *know* it was Matt Crosby?' she asked, her throat dry as she clung to the hope that it had all been a mistake...

'He gave him his card. Not that it said much. Just his name and a telephone number. He gave the same one to me when he came to the meeting last week. I've got it here somewhere,' she said, opening the briefcase she carried with her.

'It doesn't matter.' Nyssa brushed away the card Sky offered her. She didn't need any more proof that it had all been an act to get inside their organisation, keep Parker up to date on every move they made.

The tenderness, the perfect kisses that had made her feel loved, desired, a complete woman—none of them were true. She should be grateful that he'd been enough of a gentleman to leave it at that. Considering the way she'd thrown herself at him, he'd behaved like a perfect gentleman. A true knight errant.

She still wished he hadn't…

'Nyssa?' Sky was looking at her as if she was a fool, and she felt like one. She was stupid and gullible and a fool—

'Nyssa. It's me.' She flinched at the sound of a key in the door. Flinched at the sound of his voice calling out to reassure her. 'Oh. Hello, Sky. I didn't expect to see you here.'

'No, I'm sure you didn't.'

She was the last person in the world Matt had wanted to see with Nyssa. It was going to be difficult, telling her that her trusted friend had been behind the kidnap attempt. She wouldn't want to believe it. Why would she do such a thing?

'Sky went to the planning meeting,' Nyssa said. 'It's good news. The development has

been sent back for major design changes.' He
heard the flatness in her voice, saw the stiff
set of her shoulders.

'How long will that take?'

'Three months, with any luck.' She turned
to look him full in the face. 'Do you want to
phone Charles Parker and tell him? Help yourself to the phone. I presume this room is on
expenses?'

So. She knew. Sky could have only found
out from one source. He should have listened
harder to the enthusiastic young security guard
who'd fallen in love with the cinema. 'Bad
news travels fast. I'm sure he already knows.'

'You don't deny you work for him?'

He glanced at Sky. She raised her eyebrows
slightly, as if inviting him to wriggle off her
hook. 'No. I don't deny it. He employed me
to find out something, anything bad about you.
Information he could use to destroy your
Little Miss Perfect crusading reputation.'
Nyssa gave a little gasp, as if she'd still been
hoping that it might not be true. He ignored
her, keeping his gaze fixed on the other

woman in the room as he crossed the room to the telephone, picked up the receiver, punched in a number. 'After the attempt at kidnap, I gave him his money back.'

'A likely story.'

He ignored Sky's interjection, but wondered if Nyssa had noticed her lack of surprise at the word 'kidnap'.

'Parker swore he didn't organise that riot and offered to give me back my cheque if I could find out who was trying to blacken his name.'

'Oh, for heaven's sake,' Sky began loudly, 'you don't expect us to believe that!'

He no longer expected anything, except pain.

'Why not? It's at least as believable as the answer.' He tossed the camera to Nyssa. 'Check the pictures. One of them is the guy who jumped you. You'll recognise the person he's talking to. I've spent the last hour...' he paused while he sought for an appropriate word '...chatting to him.' It was Sky's turn to gasp. 'Parker?' he said as the phone was finally answered. 'It's Crosby. I've got the information you wanted—' Nyssa was pale, but Sky had turned paler, shrinking back into her chair. 'There were five people involved. I have all their names and addresses but I don't think you need worry yourself about it. They won't be causing you any more trouble.' He continued to stare at Sky and, turning the mouthpiece to his shoulder, he said, 'Will they, Sky?'

For a moment there was dead silence in the hotel room. Then Sky shook her head.

'Sky?' Nyssa's voice was oddly calm. 'What's been going on?'

Matt dropped the receiver onto the cradle and crossed to pick up his bag. 'Nyssa trusted you, Sky. Thought you were her friend. Her ally. It never occurred to her that you might be so jealous that you'd try and get her out of the way so that you could reclaim centre stage.'

'It wasn't—'

'Or was it that you found her methods a bit tame these days? Meetings with government officials just don't give you the same buzz as chaining yourself to a bulldozer, do they? And maybe she doesn't even bother to take you to those meetings.' He knew Nyssa was staring at him, but he didn't turn to meet her eyes. 'Did you think you could kill two birds with one stone? Get Nyssa out of the way and let Parker take the blame?' He walked to door. His job was done. Nyssa was safe enough. 'Cheer up. Trust is a precious thing, and I guess you've lost that, but you've been friends a long time. I'll bet even now, if you were to ask her to forgive you...'

Sky's sob rent the stillness of the room, and without a moment's hesitation Nyssa went to her, put her arms around her, held her.

'It's all right,' she murmured. 'I understand. I'm sorry, I should have seen...' He waited for a moment, but she didn't look up.

A friend might be forgiven. A lover, never.

And Matt very quietly let himself out.

Before he left the hotel he paid for their rooms, but he wouldn't be submitting an expense claim. But then he hadn't actually phoned Parker from the hotel to report his findings; he'd dialled his own number and had a one-way conversation with his answering machine.

Besides, with the planning consent on hold at the Gaumont site, the man wouldn't be able to afford his fees.

The flat seemed smaller, shabbier without Nyssa. He tossed his jacket on the sofa and a small packet slid from the inside pocket and hit the floor. He picked it up. Inside was a computer disk with a note that said simply, 'You might find this useful.' There was no signature, but it wasn't necessary. There could only be one source for such information—one of the men at James Lambert's party had been seized by an attack of conscience.

He booted up his laptop and fed in the disk. A week ago, the information stored on it would have had him singing the 'Hallelujah Chorus'. Now—

Now, instead of using it to break his enemies, wreak his revenge, he would use it to help the girl he loved.

Nyssa had kept her composure in front of Sky. Comforted her, reassured her and finally, thankfully, sent her on her way. Now she was on her own she could no longer hold back the sting of tears. She sniffed, scrabbled in her bag for a handkerchief. It was Matt's. He'd used it to dry her eyes, wipe away the tears of joy that had spilled over when he kissed her.

Joy. She flung the handkerchief in the nearest bin.

She'd felt for a few brief hours as if her whole life had slipped into place. That all the waiting had been for this moment.

Just to think of his play-acting, the pretence, was enough to dry out her eyes. He wasn't worth her tears.

How could she have been so stupid? Her very first thought after the attack had been that he was part of the plot. But then he'd held her, couched her against him, and she'd felt safe. For the first time in as long as she could remember she hadn't been alone.

She'd thought she'd been alone when her father had been killed. When her mother had remarried. When Gil had married Kitty, leaving her with her own intense, girlish passion unrequited.

On the scale of loneliness, she now knew that had been nothing.

Loving a man who, as he held you in his arms, breathed life into your frozen heart and kissed the tears from your cheeks, a man who, even as he did those things, was betraying you—that was loneliness.

She was better off lavishing her time, her fortune, her *passion* on saving neglected and unloved buildings. She could cherish them, see them brought back to life. A building couldn't betray her.

But then a building couldn't hold her in the middle of the night when she was lonely. It couldn't make her weep. Or heat her up so that her body sang with life and love.

Had it all been fake?

Matt could have destroyed Sky; instead he'd counselled forgiveness, asking nothing for himself.

Who *was* he? *Really?* And as if in answer she remembered what he'd said to her in the darkness of the garden at Delvering. *Whatever you hear, whatever anyone tells you, believe this...I will be there for you as long as you need me.*

Was that why he'd walked away. Because he thought she no longer needed him?

'Good grief, Mr Crosby, you're a stranger.' The uniformed porter regarded his jeans and denim jacket with disfavour. 'I wouldn't have recognised you.' Then, 'Are you expected?'

'No, but I'm sure His Lordship will see me.' He didn't wait for an invitation to the top floor but walked across to the high speed lift. 'Let him know I'm on my way up. I don't want to be kept waiting.'

He was met at the lift door and escorted straight into the chairman's office. 'I hoped I'd seen the last of you, Crosby.'

'All things are possible.' He placed his briefcase on the wide expanse of desk, opened it and tossed a file at the man.

'What is this?'

He had to admire the old man. He must know what was coming—he wouldn't be here unless he had dug up enough evidence to make it stick—but no one would ever have guessed from his arrogance.

'It's just a pile of paper. Statements. Computer records. Did you know that deleting records from a computer isn't enough? That they can be retrieved from apparently thin air?'

'Get on with it.'

'Very well. This is a pile of paper that could put two of your directors in jail: one of them your son-in-law. Oh, and when the cover-up you instigated is made public, you'll have to resign.' He paused. 'It'll all be downhill from there, but maybe the bank will survive. Maybe.'

'How much?'

'You don't want to check that I'm telling the truth?'

'If you'd been prepared to lie, you'd still be a director of this bank.'

'I'm glad you realise that. It makes things so much simpler.'

'How much?'

'How much is a man's reputation worth? His career?' He didn't wait for an answer. 'What price would you put on a year of his life?'

'How much?'

Matt had thought it would feel good to be in this position. It didn't. He just wanted it over. 'I want a consultant's fee to go through your records and ensure, to my own satisfaction that the fraud has been made good. I want the two directors involved to retire on the grounds of health. I want my name to stop being a dirty word.'

'Then you'd better resume your seat on the board. There'll be vacancies. And compensation.'

He'd lived a year to hear those words. He'd thought it would feel like some kind of triumph, but he'd moved on. Not in the last year, but in the last couple of weeks. 'No, thanks. I prefer working as a freelance consultant.' He smiled—he could afford to smile. 'But I'm expensive, as you'll discover.' He sat down without waiting to be invited. 'You've heard that Charles Parker is in trouble?'

'He overstretched himself. He's going to have to sell that site in Delvering at a loss.'

Matt picked up one of an array of phones. 'Call him. Make him an offer. And don't be mean.'

'Why should I do that?'

'You're going to give it me. As compensation. And for the file. No more, no less, no quibble.'

He'd shredded his files, donated his books to the nearest library and was throwing his clothes into a bag when he heard a key in the lock.

It was a bit premature of the landlord to be showing new tenants around. He wasn't due to leave until the morning. Not that it mattered. He tossed the last shirt into the bag, zipped it up. He was going now. He picked up his bag and his jacket and headed for the door. It wasn't his landlord. It was Nyssa.

'Hello, Matt.' She held up his key before putting it on the desk. 'I thought you might want this back.'

It had been a week, but the ache hadn't diminished, and to see her, like this, was as if the sun had come out after a month of rain. 'You look...' He'd been going to say wonderful, but it wasn't true. Her cheeks were hollow and her eyes were thumb-printed with dark smudges, suggesting she hadn't been getting much sleep.

She pulled a face, reading his thoughts. 'I know. I look awful, but it's been a tough week what with one thing and another.'

'I'm sorry. Truly sorry—'

'No!' Then, 'No, Matt. It's not your fault. I wanted to come sooner but Parker sold the

Gaumont the day after the planning meeting. We haven't been able to find out to whom, or what's going to happen. If I'd known I could have launched an appeal for funds. As it is—'

'You've got the cinema listed, I heard. That's a start.'

'Yes. It's a start.' They stood for a moment, just looking at one another, three feet of unbreachable space between them. 'I owe you an apology, Matt.'

'You owe me nothing—'

'Mum told me what you did. How kind you were. About the shares. Telling her instead of Parker.' He wanted to stop her, tell her that it didn't matter. That he'd do anything in the world for her. But she had to be able to walk away without any emotional baggage. 'My father bought them donkey's ages ago. To help a friend setting up a construction company.'

'It was a good investment.'

'But a bit of an embarrassment considering I was arrested for chaining myself to one of their bulldozers when they were building that motorway.'

'You were very young.'

'Eighteen. I didn't even know what it was all about. I just...well, you know all about that...'

'Yes.'

'But I don't think that would have bothered the newspapers much, do you?' She didn't wait for his answer. 'Well, obviously not, or you wouldn't have advised my mother to get them sold double-quick.' She looked up at him. 'You told me I could trust you. I'm sorry I didn't.'

'I should have told you the whole truth, right from the beginning.'

'You told Mum. You told me that last day in Delvering. I just wasn't ready to hear you. Poor Sky—'

'You feel sorry for her?'

'Don't you?'

He let it go. 'Well. No harm done.'

'Thanks to you.' The silence stretched endlessly for a few seconds...

Then Matt said, 'I've noticed you're calling Sophia "Mum" now. So you've finally forgiven her for marrying James, then?'

'Yes. You were right. She was lonely after my father died, and she really loves James and he loves her too. They deserve to be happy together—they're truly wonderful people. I'm thoroughly ashamed of the way I've been acting. But I've made my peace with them both.'

'I'm glad.'

There was another tense silence. This time Nyssa broke it. 'Are you going away?'

'Just for a short break.'

'Right. James told me that he'd offered you a job. And that you turned it down.'

'I've been offered several in the last few days. I'm suddenly Mr Popular. But I prefer working for myself.'

'Where are you going to live?'

'I've got a lease on a little place. Out of London.'

'Oh. Well, then, you're all sorted. I'm really glad for you.' She blinked, sniffed. 'Look, I have to go…' But as she quickly offered her hand, in an oddly formal little gesture, nothing could hide the gleam of tears that shimmered over the vivid blue heat of her eyes. 'Thank you, Matt. For everything.'

He ignored her hand. 'And that's it?'

'What?'

'That's how you pay your debts? With a handshake? I was promised more, Nyssa Blake. Much more.'

'But—'

His grip tightened on her fingers. 'You could have sent the key.'

'But—'

Without warning he pulled her close, so that she was jammed up tight against his chest. 'But?' he offered.

'But nothing.' She reached up with her free hand and, holding onto the front of his shirt, she kissed him, then leaned back and looked up at him with a smile that promised him the earth.

'That's better.' He released her briefly, stooped to pick up his bag, and with his arm about her waist they headed for the door.

'Where are we going?'

'To pick up your passport and then we're driving to Paris.'

'Paris? But—'

'For a weekend at the Ritz,' he said firmly. 'If we're going to finally take that shower, I think we should do it in style.'

Waking in strange places was getting to be a habit. A good habit. As Nyssa focused on the man lying beside her she thought of the memories they had made during a blissful long weekend in the city of love. Boat trips on the Seine. Walking hand in hand through the Tuilleries. Dining in small bistros.

Making love in the huge bed in a suite of totally decadent luxury at the Ritz.

It had been worth waiting for.

Matt's thick dark hair was feathered across his forehead and she reached out, brushing it back from his eyes, remembering the way he'd held her, his tenderness, his care that, for her, the first time would be special, something to remember with pleasure. For the rest of her life.

As she touched her fingers to his lips he reached up and caught her wrist, smiling as she gave a little scream of surprise. 'You're awake.'

'Ten out of ten, sweetheart. And for being so clever you get to choose your prize.'

'Can I choose anything I like?'

'Ask for your wildest dream.'

'I've already got that,' she said, grinning, and nipped at his chin.

'You are incredibly good for a man's ego, Nyssa Blake,' he said, grabbing her and rolling her onto her back.

Later, much later, lying back on the pillow with her head cradled against his chest, he said, 'We have to go home today.'

'Do we?' She snuggled against him. 'I rather like it here.'

'Yes, well, we'll do it again next year. For our anniversary.'

'The first weekend in September. I'll write it in my diary.'

'Not this weekend. Next weekend. It'll be our wedding anniversary.'

Her eyes widened. 'Excuse me? Is that a proposal?'

'It lacked something?' Matt grinned. 'Okay, how about this.' He turned to her, took her hands in his and looked directly into her eyes. 'I love you. I want you to marry me. I want you to bear my children.' Her expression was all the answer he required. 'Oh, and in your spare time there's this old cinema in Delvering that needs restoring—'

'What?'

He reached beneath his pillow and took out a long envelope. 'This is for you. I was going to drop it in the postbox as I left the flat, but this seems like a good time to give it to you. Since I don't have a ring handy.'

'What is it?'

'A token, a promise, a pledge that all that I have is yours. Body, heart and soul.' She was staring up at him. 'Open it. You'll see that I'm telling the truth.'

She ripped open the seal and as she quickly scanned the document her hand flew to her mouth. 'Tell me I'm not dreaming.'

He reached out, cradle her cheek in his palm. 'You're not dreaming.'

'But how...?' Then she gave a little cry. 'You traded this against—'

He covered her lips with his fingers, stopping the words. 'I chose this instead of revenge. I have no regrets.'

'But the deeds already have my name on them.' She looked in the envelope. 'There's no note. If I hadn't turned up on your doorstep you would have just sent them to me? Anonymously?'

He shrugged, then swore. 'Don't cry. I don't want you ever to cry again.' And he caught her to him.

'I'm not crying.' She sniffed, found a tissue, blew her nose. 'Oh, damn. Well, maybe I am crying, Matt Crosby, but only because you are such an utter and complete—' she shook her head, as if she still couldn't believe it '—*hero*.' Then, 'No, wait.' She leaned back to look up at him. 'Is *this* the little out-of-town place you mentioned?'

'Oh, yes. Didn't I say?' He grinned, couldn't help himself. 'You've got a tenant. I gave myself a ninety-nine-year lease on the top-floor flat before I assigned the deeds to you. I'm going to restore it to its original glory, and all you have to do if you want to share is I say, I will.'

'You...!'

'Yes?'

She was outraged. Charmed. Completely and utterly lost. She lay there, her hair ruffled against his arm, her eyes alight with the love she was feeling for him. 'I will, Matt Crosby. I will.'